OLD 27

Sean Siverly

OLD 27 Playlist available on Apple Music

There are so many things to be said about young love. One of the most important, enduring aspects of it is that a blossoming love knows no bounds. Great pains are taken to ensure the sown seed grows and blooms and becomes the full flower it is destined to be. However, even the most beautiful, heartiest, well-cared-for flower will eventually die. While sometimes the harshest of circumstances can be blamed for the demise, too often the best intentions---a case of over-caring---can indeed kill it. Kill it hastily, and without malice.

BOOK ONE

CHAPTER 1

When I first met Celia, she was pure and chaste. Her skin looked like porcelain: white and untarnished; smooth, cold and untouchable. She was very demure, but deep down below that innocence was an animal yearning to be freed.

She'd sweat when I held her hand. Her palm would be slick with a thin layer of perspiration. This always seemed to embarrass her. I didn't care. It was one of the many things I adored about her.

We'd dated for a couple of months before anything *major* happened between us. Our first kiss was simple and quick---almost nonchalant. Celia was embarrassed by this as well. I didn't know if her reasons stemmed from the almost nonexistent feeling of the kiss, her perceived lack of effort or *my* poor performance.

"I'm sorry," she said.

"Don't be. It's OK," I reassured her.

"I wanted to do better," she said.

"Firsts are tough," I told her. This put the blame on me. I'd done this before---I should know how it works.

"We just need to try again. We'll both be better next time," I said. "Besides, it's fun to practice." I mustered a slightly sinister grin.

Celia blushed. "That's what I've heard," she said, quickly hiding her face.

I wanted to kiss her again, but each time I'd attempt---she'd resist. I know she felt like I did, but was too shy, too embarrassed and too worried about her shortcomings to give it another go so soon---in spite of my pleading.

We did all the things that young lovers do. We'd sit on the curb outside her house at night and peer up at the stars. We'd take drives and listen to the radio or walk through the streets of town and talk. Celia's favorite thing to do was go to the park and sit on the swings. These were all things we found romantic, but they didn't seem to hurry along that 'next step.'

I refused to give up. I was so crazy about Celia and I knew the feeling was mutual. We hadn't said those *three little words* yet, but it was only a matter of time. Ironically, it might've been easier for her to tell me she loved me than to kiss me like a lover.

CHAPTER 2

We went out to dinner three nights a week. On Tuesdays we had pizza and milkshakes afterward. She always said if I bought her a milkshake, she'd give me 'sex.' It sounded weird when she'd say it. I happily obliged the tempting offer---even though I knew it was for naught.

Celia picked the meat off her pizza and set it aside. Then she pulled the cheese off in a sheet and set that aside as well. She folded the tomato sauce-laden crust in half and ate it; then finished the separated toppings. Every Tuesday I watched her perform this ritual. It was just another precious quirk of hers.

On one particular Tuesday, someone must've spiked Celia's milkshake. She asked if we could 'park.' This was something she'd never done.

"Let's go to 'The Lot,'" she said in a most sultry way.

I was taken aback by her request.

"Really?" I asked. "You want to go and park---at 'The Lot'?"

"Yes. I'm ready," she said.

"*Ready?*" I mused.

Celia knew the timbre of my voice.

"Not *that* ready," she said. "I'd like to try that kiss again, silly."

We drove to 'The Lot.' I found a secluded spot. I turned on the radio. The songs playing were terrible and did very little to enhance the situation.

"This is awful make out music," I said with a laugh.

Celia agreed.

"Sing to me," she said. "Sing me that song. The one you do

that makes me smile."

"What? That obnoxious 'Respect' thing I do?"

"That's the one. Sing it to me---but sing it to me like a ballad."

I took Celia's hands and looked into her eyes. The hazel windows to her soul sparkled as I slowly sang the lyrics to Aretha Franklin's 'Respect' to her.

I continued singing, my voice getting softer as I pulled in closer. Her eyes closed as our noses gently touched. I could feel the warm, subtle pulse of her breath as I turned my head slightly and gently pressed my lips to hers.

My eyes were opened for a second. I wanted to see Celia accept my kiss. When she had, I closed my eyes and brought her body even closer to mine.

When we stopped, I was slightly dizzy---from both a lack of oxygen and my growing affections. I wanted to believe that Celia felt the same way.

"Are you OK?" I whispered.

Celia nodded. Eyes still closed, lips parted and obviously struck by the kiss.

"I want to kiss you again," I said, gently falling toward her and not waiting for her response.

She did not resist. I could feel her reciprocating.

Our heads moved slowly as we kissed. I felt like I was in love. We hadn't pledged it yet, but it was there.

The intensity of our kiss was causing me to get an erection. It was subtle at first; however, the longer we went, the more I could feel it getting out of control. For the first time since we started dating, I thought about how much I wanted to make love with Celia.

Suddenly, something happened. Celia pulled away. She asked if we could stop.

"What's wrong?" I asked. "Did I *do* something wrong?" I feared she knew I had a hard-on.

"It's me," she said. "It feels too good."

"And that's bad?!"

"No. Well..." she paused. "I don't know. Please don't be mad."

I smiled and looked at her beautiful face. "How could I be?" I asked.

And then it happened...

"...Because I love you."

After I said the words, I felt relief that soon turned to anxiety. *Oh my God. I just told Celia I love her.*

Her eyes got big. She looked surprised, flattered and a bit scared. She was quiet. I could tell she wanted to respond; however, she just didn't know what to say.

I apologized. I knew I was going to mess things up somehow. I figured my getting an erection while we kissed would be what mortified her. I never imagined my downfall would be telling her I loved her. But here we sat: silent and unsure.

Celia smiled and took my hand. "You don't have to apologize," she said. "I think it's wonderful."

"You do?" I asked.

"Yes. I've been waiting for you to say it to me."

She looked at me, leaned in slowly and whispered, "I love you, too."

From here, we were *officially* in love and to celebrate we kissed again. This time; however, we kissed like true lovers.

We drew in simultaneously. Everything was mutual, reciprocated and we finally felt *as one.* Our mouths encircled each other's, a bit sloppily at times, but absolutely lovingly---just perfect to us. Everything we were meant to do was culminating at this moment.

I put my hands to Celia's face and touched her as we kissed. I wanted to feel her delicate features. As I caressed her, I felt the porcelain aspect of her flesh softening, becoming warmer; more human and less like a doll.

We kissed harder and I found myself losing control again. I softly pushed my tongue into her mouth. I felt her hesitation and her innocence waning with each pass of my tongue. She didn't fight me, but I knew she was confused. Each breath and gentle pant were one step closer to a place we weren't supposed to be right now. Boundaries were being broken with each second.

I blindly touched her breasts through her shirt. She shuddered but did not pull away. I was so in love with this girl and at this moment, I...

Celia stopped me. She pushed me away again. Even though I know she was feeling like I did, we could go no further tonight. At least I thought.

I loved her and ached for her so much. It was killing me. Then again, I understood her wishes and wanted to pay them the utmost respect. I succumbed to her once again. I blamed myself for any wrongdoing.

"I'm sorry," I said. "I didn't mean to do that." I was so unsure of myself.

"It's OK," Celia said. "I just didn't expect it. It was..."

"What? Give me something I can work with, here."

"It was weird," she responded. "Were you thinking of me, or someone else when you did that?"

I didn't know what to say. I *was* thinking of her. However, I was also replaying fragments of my past: the girls who could've been in this place now. Those who felt I didn't 'measure up;' those who didn't make me feel the way Celia did. Those I cared about, but who did not share my feelings. This was for what they threw away. It's what Celia salvaged and made whole again.

"Please..." I begged.

Before I could get another apology out, Celia grabbed my face, pulled me toward her and kissed me hard and deep. My tongue had no recourse for hers. She gave me twice as much as I'd given her.

She pulled back and smiled.

"There's no one else you're thinking of now, right?" she asked, looking at me hypnotically.

I stirred and said, "Um... no."

"Good. I want to know I'm all you think of."

"You are."

She looked at me and tilted her head. "Can you buy me a milkshake?" She asked. "I *really* want one."

And with that request, we left 'The Lot.' I drove very fast. It was the first time I'd ever driven so fast with Celia in the car. She did not approve.

As each day passed, Celia and I grew closer and closer. Our level of intimacy excelled. I could feel her fears about the strength of our love melting away with every touch, every kiss and new discovery. However, Celia was becoming more of the 'aggressor,' and I was finding it harder to keep up with her. I liked where things were going, but suddenly I became concerned that they were going too fast and that we may end up doing something we'd both regret. I kept these issues to myself, because I didn't know if they were truly my hang-ups, or if I was just worried about Celia.

CHAPTER 3

Senior Prom was coming very soon. Many of our friends began petitioning for Celia and me to be on the ballot for 'Best Couple.' It made us laugh. It seemed such a silly thing to be recognized for kissing behind the school during lunch or holding hands in the hallway.

"You two would be so great," one friend said.

"Yeah, but it's just so tacky," I said. "And so not us."

"But you're perfect. It would be nice to have a pair of fresh faces in this thing. It's always the same people, it seems."

Our names were mentioned to the Student Body Association for final consideration. We were rejected.

"You're a great couple, you're just *too new*," an S.B.A representative said. "Everyone likes 'the locks.' That's high school *cliquery* for you."

It was fine by us. Celia and I knew we were great together. We didn't need some hokey title, or printed piece of paper to confirm it.

"I think we're the best couple in the world---not just in our class," Celia said beaming. "We're going to show everyone how great we are."

"How will we do that?" I asked.

"We'll outlast them all. When high school is over, they'll all break up---but not us."

"Really?"

"Really! I believe it with all my heart and soul."

"How do you know?"

Celia looked into my eyes and said without hesitation, "Because you're going to marry me."

I was shocked. I didn't expect her to say anything like that, especially since we'd taken such slow and careful steps to get where we were now.

"Are you serious?" I asked.

"Why would I say it if I thought it wouldn't happen?" Celia posed.

"It just seemed pretty forthcoming. I mean, we've just gotten past the *delicate* phases of our relationship."

"But you told me you love me; that takes things to a whole new level."

"And I do."

"Well, there you go. You just said *the words*."

My head was spinning. What was going on? I was so crazy in love with this girl and she'd pledged herself to me, but we were too young to be thinking about anything beyond what we had at this moment. Marriage was very far away. Yet the more I thought about it---the more it made perfect sense.

CHAPTER 4

Celia looked absolutely divine in her prom dress. The silky, pink fabric adorned with lace accents and ruffled hems was unlike what any of the other girls were wearing. She received so many compliments and blushed heavily with each one. She and her mother had made the dress together, thus making the accolades even more special for her. I wore the standard male prom garb: a rented tuxedo. It was gray with satin-piped lining and it complemented Celia's dress almost perfectly.

When we walked to our table, I placed my hand in the small of her back and it rested effortlessly on the gradual shelf of her hip. I loved the feel of her body beneath her dress. I gently rubbed the curve of her back as I slowly guided her along. Celia smiled and told me the touch of my hand against her made her feel 'safe' and 'loved.'

I was the quintessential gentleman, not only because I was with the girl I loved and it was prom night, but because it was almost impossible not to be when you're wearing a tuxedo. I pulled Celia's chair out for her. I kept asking if there was anything she needed or anything I could do for her.

Friends joined us at our table, and even though we talked, I don't remember the conversations I just remember responding and having a few laughs. The more people that came, the less I noticed. My attention was focused mainly on Celia.

When the first song played Celia wanted to dance. I was hesitant. It was a fast song and I felt clumsy. I knew; however, that if I didn't oblige her, one of my friends just might. I didn't want that to happen. I stood up and offered her my hand. We glided to the dancefloor. As I watched my peers shuffle and weave on the parquet, I didn't feel so awkward anymore.

"I love to dance," Celia said.

"I know you do." I responded. "Our first date was at a club."

"It was, but you didn't want to dance. You just watched me."

"I remember. I'll make it up to you tonight, I promise."

"You better---you have a lot of catching up to do!"

I laughed and grabbed Celia's hand. I pulled her toward me and spun her on the dancefloor. It was a move that resembled some bygone routine. She laughed out loud at what I'd done.

"Do that again! It was so classic!" She exclaimed. "Very *Arthur Murray*."

I obliged her request. However, this time after her spin, I pulled her tightly to me and kissed her. Suddenly the music had become distant---almost ambient. Our bodies slowly twirled on the floor. I felt like we had been transported to another place.

I ran my hands softly up and down her dress. I was touching the fabric but feeling her body beneath. Celia pressed her waist hard to mine.

Once again, I could feel myself getting an erection. I tried to carefully back away, but Celia did not. She put her hands on my hips and held me tight to her. I opened my eyes while we were still kissing. I was praying to God that my hard-on couldn't be seen through the thin, gray wool of my pants.

"What's wrong?" Celia asked.

"Nothing," I said, red-faced and ashamed.

"It's *something*. You were so close; then you pulled away."

I swallowed hard and tried to think of what to say.

"I pulled something," I said with a nervous smile.

"No, you *popped* something," she responded; a sly grin growing on her face.

I dropped my head in embarrassment but had to laugh at her comment.

"I'm sorry," I said.

"Don't be. I felt it and I liked it," she said. "Did you feel *mine?*"

I was surprised by her question.

"I think so?" I said interrogatively.

Celia took my hands and pulled me close. She kissed my cheek. Even though she had placated me, I was kicking myself in the ass over my inability to control things. This was the first time she'd ever felt me hard. It seemed strange that she would welcome it, while I tried to fight it off.

I began to wonder if our differing reactions were another sign that as she became frisky, I was becoming fearful.

More than anything, I found it ironic that it happened at the prom of all places. Too many high school romances are consummated at these things, and for as much as I wanted Celia, I didn't want us to be part of *that* crowd.

We walked off the dancefloor and went to get something to eat. I was quiet. Celia was getting annoyed with my silence.

"Hello there," she said, waving her hand at me.

"I'm sorry," I said.

"Stop apologizing. It's OK. I told you that already."

"I know, but..."

"But what?"

I shook my head in slight frustration. "I don't want to rush things," I said.

Celia shook her head and smiled. "But you're not rushing things," she said. "We've been getting closer. That's what lovers do."

"I know," I said. "But a *boner* kinda' makes it seem like I'm punching the throttle."

Celia covered her mouth and giggled at the word 'boner.' She leaned in and whispered that it was a dorky word, sounding even more so being said by a man in a tuxedo. I laughed out loud at her comment. I had to agree.

"So, we're OK, then?" I asked.

"I already told you we were," she said.

"Consider the subject closed and dropped."

Celia looked at me coyly and said, "Well, not *dropped...* entirely."

Check please!

Celia and I danced to every song as if it were a slow dance. We heard our own music and set our own rhythm. I'd never felt so alive in my life. Our bodies seemed to come together. Our heartbeats synched and our love grew stronger as the night wore on. It all played like some clichéd fairy tale, but that's what the senior prom was all about and we epitomized it to the fullest.

Celia's head gently swayed between my neck and shoulder. The brush of her soft, fragrant hair against my skin was soothing and made me feel like I was the most important man in the world. I didn't want this night to end.

The DJ announced the last song of the evening: the theme song---the one we'd all been waiting to hear. This song signaled not just the end of the prom, but also the finality of high school and all its trappings and glories. After the last note faded, all we had left was graduation, the reality of adulthood and uncertain futures.

For as much as I feared the unknown, I was certain of one thing: Celia---and that certainty filled me with so much joy and hope.

We danced and kissed as the prom theme played and surrounded us. The dancefloor was full, but everyone was lost in their own world. It was as if everyone had become Celia and me. We weren't the best senior couple on paper, but everyone in the room wanted to be us at that moment.

I pulled away from Celia slightly, just enough to see her face. I wanted to tell her something---and it couldn't wait.

"Celia," I said. "Will you marry me?"

The words flowed without hesitation or pretense. I wanted this and I know she did as well. She'd said it and now I had to make it happen.

Celia's eyes brightened and began to well with tears. She was silent for a moment; then burst out, "yes!"

I felt a strange sense of accomplishment and defying of tradition: many end up making love on prom night, but does anybody ever pop the question? I smiled to myself. Through Celia's tears she asked what was so funny.

"It looks like I popped two things tonight," I said, as I grabbed her and hugged her tight.

"You did!" Celia giddily stated.

"I love you so much. Now and forever," I said.

"And forever and ever," she said. "When we leave here, will you take me for a milkshake? Maybe two?"

We left the glitz and glamor of the senior prom behind and drove to a little all-night diner. The cook and waitress smiled at us as we walked in and took a corner booth beneath a neon sign in the window.

"Brings back memories," the waitress said, as she looked over our attire.

"Hell, when I went to prom, we wore bearskins and asked our gals out by clubbin' 'em upside the head!" The cook yelled, then let out a hearty guffaw.

"What can I get you two?" The waitress asked.

I looked at Celia and then at the waitress.

"Three milkshakes, please," I said. "One chocolate, one strawberry and one vanilla."

"Three?" The waitress asked.

"Yes, ma'am. One for her, one for me and one to share. We're celebrating."

The waitress smiled and winked at us.

"Y'all are just too adorable." She looked at Celia and pointed to me. "This one's a keeper, honey."

Celia blushed and said, "Don't I know it!"

CHAPTER 5

Prom was over, Celia said 'yes,' and I was back to work. My job was simple: park, wash and fuel up cars on a sales lot. Nothing to get in a tussle about, but that's what I was doing.

"You're here, but you're not *here*," my boss said.

I was *trying* to focus on work.

"I know. I've got too much on my mind," I said. "I'm sorry. I'll pull it together."

My boss clapped my shoulder. "It's cool," he said. "You're a couple of days from graduating. I know what that's like. Why don't you fill up the cars on the end lot, then cut loose for the day?"

"Really?" I asked. "I don't want to blow off the day, just because I'm being flighty."

"It's no big deal," my boss said. "If I need you---I'll call you."

I drove the cars one-by-one from the end lot to the gas station and back to the end lot. The thought of getting off work early was bittersweet. I felt like I was letting my boss down and shirking my responsibilities.

After fueling the last car and returning to the lot, I sat for a moment and took in my surroundings. I was in a brand-new car---one I could drive, wash and fuel up but not afford to buy. I was enthralled by the 'new car smell.' I wondered how come only new vehicles smelled this way---so unique. It also made me wonder about the scents of life in general: how love has such a sweet fragrance, while anger and hate smell like rotten garbage or rancid meat.

I didn't want to get out of the car. Leaving these comfortable, wonderfully aromatic environs would mean stepping out into the uncertainties I'd feared. Oh my God---was I ready for what lie ahead? Moreover, was I ready to drag Celia down into the doldrums with me? What was I going to do?

I pulled myself together and got out of the car. The outside air smelled stale. I took one last deep breath of the car's interior.

I headed back to the sales office and my boss greeted me with a fifty-dollar bill and some instructions: "Go take this pretty lady out to dinner," he said, pointing to Celia. She was sitting in a chair next to the boss's desk.

I smiled when I saw her. I could feel my worries begin to float away.

"Well, where did you come from?" I asked.

"My mom had to do some shopping," she said. "So, she dropped me off."

I hugged Celia tightly. I was so glad to see her. She felt good in my arms. It was like I hadn't seen her in weeks.

My boss gave me a pager and told me to 'get.' I didn't hesitate. I thanked him for the 'advance' on the way out. He smiled and waved me off like it was no big deal.

Celia and I spent the day planning how we would spend our evening. We drove all over but ended up going nowhere; sometimes that was the best place to be. She had made a lunch for me. We shared it at one of our insignificant stops.

"What would you like to do tonight?" Celia asked as she fed me a potato chip.

"I don't know. We could go to a movie," I suggested half-heartedly.

"You don't want to go to a movie again, do you?" She asked. "What's to see?"

"There's got to be something."

She wasn't convinced.

"Why don't we go to dinner and then we can think about it," Celia said. "Does that sound good?"

"That works for me," I said. "It's Tuesday. The usual?"

Celia shook her head. "No. Not tonight," she said. "Let's break tradition. I want you to take me out for a *real* dinner. It is our 'anniversary,' you know."

For a second I was lost; then I realized it had been a week since prom night and since I'd popped the question.

"Where do you want to go?" I asked. "Just name it."

"How about we go someplace romantic?" Celia suggested. "A place with candles and cloth napkins; a place where you'd take your true love."

I gave her a contemplative look. "An *expensive* place, you mean," I said.

"Well, not expensive---but not cheap either," she said. "Nice. Nice and fancy. But affordable, too."

"I think we can do that," I said, with an obliging nod.

I dropped Celia off at home and I told her I'd be back around seven PM. Seven seemed like the right time to go out to a swank place. She kissed me through the open driver's side window and watched as I drove away. I kept looking in the rearview mirror, glancing back at her until her form had disappeared into the distance.

I thought about how much I loved her and how I wanted to make this dinner special. Here I was: in love and semi-engaged. I wanted everything to be just right and I had some extra money in my pocket to help things along. I shouldn't be worried about a damn thing, but unfortunately, every damn thing was what worried me.

As I drove home, I had a sudden thought flash in my head and when it hit---it struck like lightning: *I wanted to buy Celia a ring.* I'd asked her to marry me, but that was prom talk, if I was going to make it real, I had to put a diamond on her finger. Was I really thinking about this? Moreover, was I really going *to do* this?

Yes. Yes, I was...

I drove to the first place I could think of that would have

diamond rings that I could afford---I went to a pawn shop. I felt like a cheapskate and even a little sleazy venturing into the store, but they had what I wanted, and it was well within my financial means.

As I looked at the rings my mind bounced in different directions. What would Celia think if she knew I'd bought her ring here and not at a real jewelry store? What the hell are my parents going to say about it? What about Celia's parents?

Both our folks already thought I tended to err on the side of irresponsibility, and this was definitely not the soundest decision---even though it made perfect sense to me.

I began to answer each of my questions as I continued perusing the fare: Celia won't know it's from a pawn shop if I don't tell her; I'll just clean it up nice and present it to her at dinner. She'll love it and someday I'll be able to afford a better, nicer---non-pawn shop---one.

As for our parents, I figured they didn't have to know anything at this point. We'd tell them eventually. Right now, none of that mattered. I was going to do this---*for better or worse.*

The pawnbroker was a crusty geezer. He looked pissed off and impatient. I couldn't decide which ring I liked the best. There were several to choose from.

"Make a pick yet, Romeo?" The pawnbroker growled.

"Nope. I'm thinking I may take my money elsewhere," I said, giving him an indecisive look.

Suddenly, the pawnbroker's whole demeanor changed. He went from geezer to pleaser, pulling out the trays of rings from behind the glass case and telling me the virtues of each one. I really hadn't planned on bailing, but my bluff helped make the experience a tolerable one.

I described Celia's fingers to the pawnbroker. I told him they were slender and smooth; delicate and pale. I leaned towards rings with thinner bands and subtle diamonds, but something that did stand out; something she'd never want to take off. After several minutes of looking, I'd found it.

"I'll take that one," I said, pointing to a gold band that seemed to twist where the diamond sat.

"Nice one," the pawnbroker said, "It's unique without being overstated."

I agreed with his assessment. I couldn't see the price tag hanging off the band.

"How much do you want for it?" I asked.

The pawnbroker looked at me, then at the ring. He picked up the tag and shook his head. I wasn't sure what to make of this.

"What's wrong?" I asked.

"This can't be right," he said.

"What? Is it too much?"

"Yeah, it's way too much. I must've mismarked it or something."

I didn't let on that I had the money. I didn't have a lot, but I did have enough. I let him cut his own price. I was hoping for a good deal.

"Kid, I like ya'," the pawnbroker said. "How's one-fifty sound to ya'?"

"Sold," I said.

I paid for the ring and the pawnbroker found a purple, velvet box to put it in. He dusted off the box, pulled the tag from the ring and set it aside. He placed the ring into the white, padded insert. It fit perfectly.

"Like Cinderella and her shoe," he said.

"Just like that," I replied.

I grabbed my purchase and put it in my pocket.

"Ya' need a receipt?" The pawnbroker asked.

"No. This isn't coming back," I said with a smile.

The pawnbroker put the rings back into the case and thanked me for my business. I told him it had been a pleasure.

As I made my way out, I spied the price tag he'd taken off the ring: *two-hundred fifty dollars.* He'd saved me a c-note but cost him one as well. I felt a little guilty at first, but then chalked it up to a wellspring of good fortune all around. Now, I just needed to find a place for Celia and me to eat and make this official.

When I got home it was nearing five PM. I had a short amount of time to get ready, while simultaneously fielding questions from my folks about my day.

I said my day was fine and my boss let me go early; then I ran some errands.

My dad asked if I was going out tonight and I told him I was.

My mom asked where I was going. I almost spilled my guts about the fancy dinner. I lied and said we were doing our usual Tuesday.

"That girl sure does love pizza," my mom said.

"She does," I replied. "I don't know how she stays so thin."

I didn't want to talk. I was in a hurry to get cleaned up, but played along as best I could, while watching the clock. At almost six PM, I made haste.

CHAPTER 6

Celia and I drove quietly to our as yet to be determined dining location. She seemed nervous, but her anxiety level couldn't even be close to mine. My heart was pounding and even with the air conditioner on, I could feel the bullets of sweat ready to launch from my brow at any second.

"What did you do after I left today?" I asked.

"Nothing really," Celia said. "I just thought about what we'd do tonight; then I beat my brothers in a game of Skip-Bo. What did you do?"

"Oh, I just drove around and did a couple of things; nothing as exciting as Skip-Bo, though."

Celia suddenly clapped her hands together like an excited child. "So where are we going to eat for our anniversary?" She asked.

I still wasn't sure, so I blurted out, "I'm taking you to the Sheraton."

Celia seemed overly ecstatic about this. It was just a restaurant, but it was in a nice hotel, it *did* have candles and cloth napkins and it was *definitely not* pizza.

We arrived at the Sheraton and made our way to the restaurant. Although we were both dressed well enough to dine at such an establishment, the maître d' seemed less than impressed with us.

"Do you have a reservation?" He asked with a slight huff.

"No, I didn't think we'd needed one," I said.

"Well, sir, we do have a protocol and reservations are *highly* recommended."

"But not *absolutely* necessary, right?"

The maître d' huffed again.

I looked around the restaurant and saw plenty of empty tables.

"Really? I should've called ahead?" I asked. "Even on such a slow night?"

The maître d' shook his head as if to say: 'silly boy, we're expecting a full house at any moment.'

I needed this place to be where we ate, and where I gave Celia the ring. Yes, it was spontaneous, but it was also perfect. This snitty bastard *had* to give us a table, so I played the 'special occasion' card.

"Is there anything you can do?" I asked. "This is a very special night for us."

He looked at us like we were too young to have such nights yet.

"Oh, and what is the occasion?" He asked.

"It's our anniversary," I said. "And we wanted to spend it here, tonight."

He still had a suspicious look on his face, but the maître d' stepped back and grabbed two menus. He showed us to a lovely, intimate table for two---complete with a red, glass candle sheathed in stretchy, white plastic netting in the center; mono-grammed cloth napkins rolled around the shiniest silverware I'd ever seen and a fancy tablecloth to complete the ensemble.

I looked at Celia. Her face was so beautiful in the soft glow of the candlelight.

"Sorry about that guy," I said. "Part of the charm, I guess."

Celia said nothing. She just smiled.

We looked over our menus. There were many things on there that neither of us had heard of. Perhaps the idea of a fancy dinner was better suited for the fantasy realm?

"Find anything that sounds good?" I asked.

"No," Celia said, coldly. "Maybe we should've gone for pizza."

"We still can, you know. We haven't ordered yet."

"I want to order something, but I don't know what half of this stuff is."

"Me either, but we could ask. I can tell you a few things."

Celia put her menu down, reached across the table and took my hands into hers.

"Even though this place is not what I expected---*you* are. I love you so much," she said.

"I love you, too," I said. "More than you could know."

"Maybe we're too simple for a place like this," she said. "Maybe we're destined for pizza every Tuesday and pork chops on Thursday---who knows?"

I smiled at Celia's observation. "Simple is good," I said. "It makes things easier."

"Let's order something," Celia said. "Tell me what I might like."

I read over the menu and came across a couple dishes that I knew. I suggested filet mignon for a beef dish, or chicken cordon bleu. I gave a quick explanation of each and they both seemed to appeal to Celia. She was especially intrigued when I told her the filet mignon had a bacon-wrap option.

"I'm impressed with your knowledge of *snooty* food," Celia said sarcastically.

"It's a gift," I said. "My folks go out a lot and I get to hear about things."

"Very classy!"

"Indeed. And I've eaten cordon bleu."

Celia seemed surprised. "You have?!" She asked.

"Yeah, it's a breaded piece of chicken stuffed with ham and cheese," I said. "It's pretty good."

Celia thought for a moment and made her decision.

"I'll have the cordon bleu," she said, over accenting the word *bleu.*

The waiter came by and took our drink orders. We both ordered ginger ales and shrimp cocktails for appetizers. The drinks came first, then the appetizers. As we ate the cold, savory, wrinkled crustacean tails, we looked at each other and hardly said a word.

The waiter returned to take our dinner orders. We both ordered the cordon bleu.

"Why does it take so long to get your food in a place like this?" Celia asked.

"I don't know," I said. "It must be so you can enjoy the atmosphere or something. Are you bored?"

"No, just hungry. I liked the shrimp. It's going to give us bad breath."

I laughed. "Probably," I said. "But we both carry a lot of gum."

Our food finally arrived. Celia tried to be as prim and proper as she could, but she was starving. Her country table manners came to the fore.

"Slow down, Celia." I said, gently patting my hand on the table.

"I'm just so hungry and this is really good!" She said, hastily putting a piece of chicken into her mouth.

"Well, then take a minute to enjoy it."

"Next you're gonna' tell me to eat with my fork *and* knife like a European."

"No, I won't do that---that's even too fancy for me!"

Celia and I both shared a laugh and the pace of our meal slowed. We talked between bites and took in our surroundings. Neither of us had ever been to a place like this and for as much of a hassle as it seemed to get a table, we wanted to enjoy the experience and be *one of them* for an evening.

All of this was definitely easing the situation for me to propose to Celia. I watched her eat and even though she kept returning suspicious glances, I was convinced she had no idea what was about to occur.

The waiter returned when we'd finished and asked if we'd enjoyed our meals. We had indeed. He asked if we were going to have dessert and handed us two small menus. He said he'd be back to take our order when we'd decided.

I didn't know what to get, if anything. Celia did want a

dessert but didn't know what. She suggested we share something.

"Do you like cheesecake?" She asked.

"I do," I said. "But I'd rather have something else."

"Oh. What's this? Sore-*bet?*"

"It's pronounced: sore-*bay*. It's like a fruity, ice cream---a fancy sherbet, really."

"That sounds nice. Let's get that---strawberry!"

The waiter took our dessert order and within a few minutes we were staring at a crystal goblet with a perfectly, round dollop of pink, glistening, strawberry sorbet. Two small spoons were evenly placed on opposite sides of the vessel, their handles resting in the grooves of the lipped rim of the goblet. It looked too beautiful to eat.

As we stared at the sorbet, the maître d' came around to our table and asked how our evening was going so far. I told him it had been fine. He still seemed peeved with us. I was getting the feeling that he thought he'd been hoodwinked into letting two love-struck teenagers usurp one of his tables for the night.

"We're just about to enjoy this delicious sorbet," I said with a cynical grin.

He said nothing, just nodded and moved to another table---one of only a few that was occupied.

"I don't like that guy," Celia said. "He's just too..." she paused. "Uptight and stuff."

I laughed and said, "Yeah, but to have his job, you gotta' have a stick up your ass, I suppose."

Celia laughed and snorted. It was not the type of thing you'd *ever* expect to hear in a place like this, but it was adorable, refreshing and *so her*. As strange as it seems, after that, I couldn't wait any longer. It was time to put on a show for the maître d' and make Celia's dream come true.

I got up and walked to her chair. At first, she seemed confused, but then reality began to set in. I stood above her and looked into her eyes before I lowered myself down onto my right knee. Celia started shaking. Tears began to build in her eyes. I hadn't even said a word yet. I began shaking as well.

This was something I wanted so much, but that also carried so many unknowns. I reached in my pocket and took out the ring box. Celia was on the verge of saying 'yes' before I'd opened it. I popped the top back and the glow of the candlelight made the ring look even more beautiful than it was. She stared at the ring; her eyes darting between it and my eyes.

I removed the ring from the box and held it up so she could see that it wasn't some fake prop to get her hopes up. I softly took her left hand, kissed it and spoke:

"Celia. So far, our journey has been short, but I know we're destined for eternity," I said. "You've made me so happy; shown me so much love and made me want to be the best man I can be. You make me whole. Before you, there was nothing, but since we've met, I've felt fulfilled, but I don't have all I need in my life---until now."

I slowly placed the ring on Celia's finger.

"Now," I said. "I know I can be complete. Will you marry me?"

A squeal burst from Celia, as did a well of tears. She jumped from her chair, grabbed me tightly and whispered into my ear, "Yes! Yes! Yes!"

I jokingly told her she needed to let everyone else know, as well.

"YES!" She shouted. "Without a doubt---*YES!*"

The maître d' came and congratulated us and told the waiter to give him the check. Our sorbet had melted, but that was OK. I think after this, we were definitely going for milkshakes.

We drove from the Sheraton as an officially engaged couple. I felt like the happiest person in the world and I had to think that Celia shared that sentiment. She kept looking at her ring. Every so often I wondered if she was staring at it because of what it symbolized, or because she'd figured out that I'd bought it a pawn shop.

"You've made me so happy... I just..." she said, stuttering.

"Just know how much I love you, Celia," I said. "That's all that matters."

"When you asked me at the prom, I felt how real it was, but this... this makes it..."

I continued her thought, "...official?"

"Yes. 'Official.' That sounds so weird, but it's so true!" Celia said, as she began to cry again.

So much had happened, but the night was still young. We weren't ready to go home, so I asked her what she would like to do. I figured she'd want to go and get the traditional 'I'll give you sex' milkshake, but she didn't bring it up. She looked at her ring again before turning to me.

"Earlier today when we were talking about what to do tonight, you acted weird. Was this why?" Celia asked.

I answered her honestly. "No. I didn't even think about this ring until I drove home after I dropped you off," I said. "It was completely spontaneous; even more so than the restaurant."

She smiled and shook her head. "I never know what you're going to do," she said.

"Me neither," I replied.

"So, what *did* you want to do tonight? It had to be something, if nothing we'd done in the last couple of hours was planned."

I took a deep breath. I still wasn't sure how to word what I wanted to tell her. Then I was hit once again with a flash like the one that directed me to buy her ring. I found a turnout and pulled my car off the road and parked it. Celia was surprised by this, but I didn't think I could say what I wanted while I was driving.

I turned to her, put my hands to her face and caressed her soft cheeks. I leaned in and kissed her. She reciprocated and we kissed deep and slow. After about a minute, I told her what I'd been thinking.

"I want to spend the night with you," I said.

Celia sat silent, mouth agape and in a state of soft shock. I couldn't tell if it was the residual effect of our kiss or what I'd just said, so I asked her if she was OK.

"Yeah, I'm fine," she said bluntly.

Her reaction made me feel like I needed to apologize to her again.

"I'm so sorry," I said. "I know you're not ready for that."

Celia looked at her ring again. "Not tonight," she said. "But it's going to happen sooner than you think."

I could feel a confident grin spreading across my face, but I tried as best I could to hide it from Celia. It was no use; she saw it and she too had a similar expression.

"Maybe we could just go someplace and be together---a little more than normal," I said.

"What do you mean?" Celia asked.

"Let's go to 'The Lot' and I'll show you."

She suddenly became guarded, again. I could sense a slight curiousness in her eyes, but she was not certain what to expect. I tried to explain that everything would be above board, and nothing would get pushed 'too far.' That was easier said than done, since Celia had become more adventurous of late. All we could do was see where things led and if they got out of hand, we'd know to stop.

We drove to 'The Lot' and parked. The last time we were here, the music on the radio sucked, but tonight I'd found a nice station and it provided the perfect background ambiance for us to take our next step forward.

I leaned over to kiss Celia and it was as if we'd continued our roadside kiss. We started slow and soft, but as we progressed, we became more passionate---almost savage and violent. We'd never kissed like this before and the sheer intensity was forcing blood to fill my penis again. My erection was strong and felt like it was going to burst my zipper.

As we kissed, I took my shirt off and Celia touched my chest. She rubbed my skin and hair; timidly gliding her fingers over me. She kissed my neck, sucking hard on the skin. The suction of her mouth drew deep into my flesh---I was definitely going to have a hickey after this.

I reached my hands into Celia's blouse and felt her breasts through her bra. Her nipples were hard. I wanted to feel them outside of the lacy fabric. I kissed her neck to entice her.

"Please, can we take your bra off?" I begged. "I want to feel you."

Celia pulled away panting.

"OK," she said. "But nothing else comes off---promise?"

"I promise."

Celia pulled her blouse off and reached behind her back to unhook her bra. She pushed the straps down off her shoulders and I finished for her.

I stared lovingly at her small, pert, but perfect breasts. I felt her up, gently stroking and massaging her chest. Her pink nipples were so hard and sensitive to my touch. I didn't think about anything else but running my tongue over every inch of the pale, protruding mounds on her chest.

Celia panted and moaned, whispering how good it felt.

"What does it feel like?" I asked, concerned and curious.

"I can't describe it," she said. "But it makes me feel so... special."

"*Special?*"

"Yeah... like... it's all for me. Like... I can't..."

As strange as it sounded---I understood completely.

I moved myself over and slid underneath her. Celia was now straddling me; our bare chests rubbing against each other.

Celia wrapped her legs around my waist and moved against me. She could feel my erection through my pants but continued to move back and forth over it.

"This feels so incredible," she whispered as I continued to kiss her chest.

"I want you..." I said under my breath.

Celia asked me to repeat myself, as if she wasn't sure what she'd heard.

"I want you," I whispered. "I want to make love to you right now. Let me make love to you, Celia... please."

Then it happened---I'd gone 'too far' once again.

Celia turned away and asked me to take her home. This was something new. Any other time I'd pushed the envelope, we just stopped, but for some reason, telling her I wanted to make love not only pushed the envelope, but sent it flying.

Celia dressed herself quietly while I watched in shame and disbelief.

"Oh my God, I'm so sorry," I said. "I didn't..."

Celia stopped me.

"Don't say it," she said softly. "Don't say anything, OK."

I made a zipping motion across my mouth and threw away the invisible key. I hated this. I hated when these things happened to us. We would get so far and then---BAM! A white light of innocence would burst through and blind us. I couldn't help but wonder, though: if Celia had initiated this, would we have gone all the way? Who the hell knows?

I drove Celia home shirtless and in silence. There were so many things I could've said, but I promised to keep it 'zipped.' I was hoping that Celia would express an opinion, but that didn't happen. For the first time since we started dating, we were completely distant. What a hell of a way to begin an engagement.

We pulled into her driveway at about two AM. It was a new day for us, but an uncertain one at that. I tried to apologize once again, but Celia didn't want to hear it. I was so confused: we were officially engaged; we blew away the other couples in our class; were so close to making love and then... *whatever.*

I reached for her hand as she got out of the car.

"Can I see you tomorrow?" I asked, doubtful and almost in tears.

"I think so," she said. "We need to talk."

I shook my head. "I don't like how that sounds," I said.

Celia sighed. "Don't worry," she said. "It's not as bad as you think."

"Why does it seem that way?" I asked.

"Because you worry too much. You know I love you. I'm just not ready. I got scared."

"I understand."

"Good. I just want everything to be right---don't you?"

"Yes, definitely."

"Then give me time. I promise it'll be worth it."

And with those words, Celia closed the car door and walked up to her house. I was so confused and upset with myself. I didn't know what to do; I didn't know what I'd done besides say what was on my mind. Celia and I had been dating for several months and I still couldn't figure her out. She ran hot and cold, but then again---I had been as well, I suppose. The only thing I knew for certain was that I needed to put on my shirt.

I drove home and when I got to my house, I sat silently in my car for a while. The sky was beginning to lighten with the dawn of the new day. I was so tired. I wasn't sure if I had to work today or not, but I didn't care. All I cared about was the fact that I'd messed things up with Celia and that I was still packing a painful erection. I needed to relieve my stress.

I went into the bathroom and masturbated like I hadn't done in quite a while and when I finally ejaculated, I felt like I was going to faint. It was so painful, but so pleasurable, too. *Oh my God---I needed to make love to Celia so bad.* I needed her to feel how powerful my love for her was physically as well as emotionally.

CHAPTER 7

I woke up to the sound of my work pager buzzing on my desk. I half-blindly stumbled over to look at it. I shut it off, threw on a pair of sweatpants and went to call work.

I made my call and lucky me---I had the day off. I needed it. There were too many things I had to face today and none of them gave me a good feeling.

I went to take a shower and hoped the hot water beating on my skin would help to ease my stress a little. It didn't, but at least I was getting clean.

After I finished grooming and preening, I went to call Celia. So much happened last night and even though I feared the worst, I thought that hearing her voice---no matter what she said---would be a nice way to get the day started.

Her phone rang and rang but there was no answer. It was around eleven AM, so I figured someone had to be home. I tried again. No answer. I dialed her prefix, said *forget it,* and hung up the handset. I decided to go for a drive and maybe stop by and see a couple of friends.

As I drove, I replayed last night. It was a mess from the start. Sure, there were fantastic highlights but from the moment I picked Celia up, things were already doomed. Was I an idiot for buying her that ring? *No. It was the right thing to do.* I wanted to show I was committed. Looking back, maybe I *should be* committed. What the hell?

Maybe that snit maître d' was right in his scoffing us? *What does he know?* I know I love Celia and she loves me. Why can't I keep my big mouth shut? *I want to make love to you...* why did I say that? *Because it's true, you moron.* I'm so confused.

I began to wonder if Celia told her parents, or if they saw the ring. That would be grounds for trouble. I should have waited. I should have asked her dad first, or something---is that even a thing anymore? Oh my God, this is so screwed up.

I stopped to see my friend David. He was outside working on his car. I parked, got out and walked toward him. He didn't see me.

"You busy?" I asked, sarcastically.

He looked up from under the hood and seemed flustered.

"Kind of," David said. "But I'd be lying if I said I was getting anything done."

"What are you doing?"

"Trying to change my spark plugs, but I can't get them out."

"Why not? They too tight?"

"No, I can't get the socket to stay on the plug."

"Don't you have a plug socket?"

"No. What's that?"

"It's a socket with a piece of rubber in it that grips the plug, so it won't slip."

David looked at me like I was both a genius and an idiot.

"Well, if I had one, I'd know what it was," he said. "I would've been done an hour ago! Do you have one on you?"

"Probably," I said. "Let me check."

I had one, but if I got it out, I'd have to help change the plugs. I didn't want to do that. It's not that I didn't want to help, I just didn't feel like getting greasy, and these plugs were in a location that was almost impossible to get to without some clever maneuvering and special tools, and...

I stopped and stood for a second.

David yelled to me, "You got one?"

"Yeah..." I answered but sounded uncertain and mumbled incoherently. "...it's a five-eighths inch... I have to go..."

"Dude! The socket!" He yelled again. "Can I borrow it?"

I said nothing. I grabbed the socket and tossed it toward him. It landed in the grass by his car.

"Where are you going?" David asked, as he picked up the socket. "Aren't you going to stay and watch me struggle with this?!"

"No, I can't. But you just helped me fix something!" I yelled to him as I got in my car and headed home.

As I drove, I thought about the exchange between David and me. I thought about how he was having trouble fixing his car because he needed a 'special tool' to do the job. With Celia, I'd always known that I was dealing with a special case. Celia was different than other girls I'd been with. She required handling and attention that was unique. I *did* realize this. However, it took David to reinforce the fact.

As soon as I returned home, I called Celia again. I dialed her number and the phone just rang and rang. Where the hell could she be? Why wasn't anyone there to answer? Something was wrong. No---*everything* was wrong. I wanted to drive over and see her. She said we needed to talk today anyway, so why not just go to her house? It took every ounce of energy I had to quell the urge, but I did resist. I threw myself into a chair by the phone and waited---impatiently---for something to happen. Nothing did.

I spent the next two days in a fog of uncertainty and depression. What had I done to make Celia just cut me off with not even a 'goodbye,' or a 'fuck you'? I began to hate myself and everything that I thought was good, right and just.

My boss kept me busy running the new models through the carwash and it was probably the best thing for me. It kept my mind off of Celia; however, I'd finally reached my breaking point and instead of going to the carwash, I threw caution to the wind, diverted direction and drove a brand-new Plymouth *Gran Fury* to Celia's house to get some answers.

I pulled into her driveway and her dad---who everyone called *Big Kenny*---was outside with a disgruntled look on his face.

"You steal that boat?" He asked.

"Kind of, sir. It's a work car," I said. "Is Celia home? I've been trying to call her for the last couple of days." I wanted to cut the chatter short.

"She's around. I don't know where, though." He said bluntly. "You can check the house."

I ran to the front door and opened it. I called Celia's name and got no answer. I walked into the house and called to her again. Still nothing. What the hell was going on?

"CELIA! GODAMMIT! WHAT THE HELL ARE YOU TRYING TO DO TO ME?!" I yelled, as I stood in hallway between her bedroom and the dining room.

Celia's dad heard me yelling and stormed in to find out why.

"Jesus Christ, boy---what the hell are you yelling about?!" He asked.

"Sir, I have to see Celia," I said. "I haven't talked to her in days."

"She's been here the whole time, don't know what could be keeping her from you," he said. He sounded like he was trying to console me.

Celia came out of the bathroom. She was in a bathrobe and was toweling off her wet hair. She wasn't wearing any makeup and looked so different. I'd never seen her without any sort of 'glamorama'---as she called it---before.

My first thought was that she had spent the last few days in the shower washing my gropes and slobbering from her body---one explanation as to why I hadn't heard from her.

My mind jumped rails and I began to think she had some other guy in her bedroom and was showering because they'd just *finished up.* Where that thought came from, I don't know, but it became more prevalent as I stood watching her in her bathrobe. *Explains a lot* I presumptuously said to myself.

Celia's dad left us alone, but not before mentioning I was driving 'a big, red boat.'

Celia shook her head in confusion. "What is he talking

about?" She asked.

"I've got a car from work," I said. "I'm supposed to be washing it."

"Are you going to get in trouble for being gone so long?" She asked.

"I could get *fired.* I'm kind of stealing the car; it ain't being washed and it ain't on the lot... it's AWOL and so am I."

"Oh no..."

"Oh *yeah.* I don't care though. I had to see you. I've been missing you so much."

I stepped toward her and held out my arms to hug her.

Celia pulled the towel she'd used to dry her hair over her shoulders and cinched her robe tight. Her gesture made me feel horrible. It was as if she was telling me not to touch her and that she had been violated.

"What's the matter?" I asked, shocked.

"Nothing," she said unconvincingly. "I've just been thinking about the other night. So much happened."

I nodded in agreement. "Yeah... a lot did happen," I said. "You left me with my head reeling and a million questions as to what I'd done wrong. I thought everything was OK."

"It was. You made me feel... well... like I've never felt before. I came home that night and I didn't know what to make of any of it."

"Neither did I---especially the way it all ended. And since I hadn't heard from you, I thought *we'd* ended," I stated. I sounded a bit hostile.

Celia picked up on my dig. "That's not being fair," she retorted. "I was just confused about how things went. I'm still not sure..."

I cut her off.

"What are you 'not sure' about?" I asked. "My God, Celia, you have to know how much I love you." I lowered my voice. "We're engaged; we're taking steps toward our future together---what's to be unsure about?"

Celia did not hesitate to answer. "Everything," she said.

I didn't know what to say. In all honesty, I couldn't disagree with her, but I wasn't willing to give up.

"Don't you believe in us?" I asked.

Celia shook her head in disbelief. "My God, how could you even ask such a thing? Of course, I do!" She snapped. "I believe in us more than I believe in anything. I want this. I want you. I want *US!*"

I knew she was sincere, but I had to know that *she* knew it, too. I had to do the one thing I'd tried to avoid: I had to spray the conversation with testosterone.

"Prove it," I demanded. "Spend the night with me."

"I can't," she whispered emphatically.

"Can't... or won't."

"You're making this so hard for me."

"That's the idea. It's not supposed to be, but you put me in a tailspin. When I left you the other night we were going to 'talk,' and then nothing. I can't make this easy for you, because it hasn't been easy for me. It's tearing me apart."

"Can I make a deal with you?" Celia asked.

"Sure," I said.

She stepped toward me and leaned in close.

"Graduation night. High school will be over, and our new lives will begin," she whispered seductively. "That's when we'll spend the night together. I promise. I promise this---*and me*---to you, as well."

I stood silent and stunned. I just looked at her.

"I want to make love to you, too," Celia said. "I wanted to the other night. I just wasn't ready-*ready*.

"It's some stupid thing with girls. I don't know if it's the pregnancy thing, or fear of getting dumped, or both, but I'm old-fashioned. I'm cautious and I want everything to be perfect before I give myself to anyone. But what I *do* know for sure is this--- I want *you* to be my first."

"I want that too," I said. "Your first and last and always."

"That sounds so romantic."

"It's the title of a Sisters of Mercy album."

"How Goth."

For the first time in the last couple of days, I laughed.

Celia smiled and hugged me tightly. I felt the tension falling away. I stroked her shoulders and slowly ran my hands down her back. I felt her curves through her robe. She didn't resist in any way as I brought my hands to the front and slipped them inside, feeling her naked skin beneath.

I moved down and felt her silky panties. I softly touched the fabric and could feel hints of her pubic hair beneath. I slowly slid my middle finger between her legs and could feel she was wet. She threw her head back and groaned quietly as I pushed my finger harder between her legs; opening her vulva and pressing the smooth silk of her underwear against it. She let out a hastened sigh and a gasping breath---then whispered for me to stop. I did just as she asked.

"Oh my God... no more," she whispered. "It's just a few more days."

Celia pulled away from me. She gathered herself. It felt as if we'd been caught committing a crime. She kissed me and told me I needed to get back to work. She was right. I was an hour off schedule, but I didn't care. What just happened between us was all I'd cared about; any other consequences would be---*inconsequential.*

Celia got dressed and walked me out to the car. She giggled at the gargantuan size of it.

Celia's dad asked about the mileage.

"I've had to fill it up twice since I've been here, sir," I joked.

He looked at Celia. "Sugar," he said. "You've got to keep this guy."

Celia concurred: "I plan to daddy!"

CHAPTER 8

Graduation night came faster than I thought it would. Celia and I had purposely kept our contact to a minimum. It was a way to build up the anticipation. I was nervous. Actually, *nervous* didn't cut it---I was scared to death. It wasn't because I was 99.9% sure I was going to make love with Celia tonight; it was because *this was it*---my invincible days of being an insouciant high schooler were about to end.

Sure, I had a job and responsibilities already, but I was about to become an adult. From here it was the real stuff: make-or-break decisions that could lead you to either success or just *suck*.

For the last couple of years, my folks were pulling me in different directions. My mom wanted me to be the sensitive *artiste* and go to college. She wanted me to paint and follow in the footsteps of Pablo Picasso or write and become the next Ernest Hemingway. My dad; however, thought I needed to 'man up,' get my head straight, assimilate to structure and join the military. They both had merits, but the more I thought about each option, the more I thought they equally sucked.

I didn't have the attention span, or the patience for college---even an art college; although the arts were my thing. Similarly, I was definitely not service material. Mindless, robotic orders, people yelling and calling me names while trying to dehumanize me were not things I fared well with, either. I was also a bit of a pacifist.

I chose the least worst of the choices and opted to go to college. Either way, it was a two to four-year commitment to something I wasn't ready to make at the moment---at least not of my own accord. The worst part was that it would separate me from Celia. It would only be temporary, but a separation, nonetheless.

As I got myself dressed and ready to leave for the graduation ceremony, my mind focused on the events to take place post-commencement. The only thing I was sure of was that since this was Celia's first time I would have to be gentle, careful and attentive to her every wish. She was giving me the gift of her virginity and I wanted to be certain I treated it with the utmost care, respect and honor.

Tonight, is going to be amazing, I said to myself.

However, Celia's and my night would have to wait a little longer to begin. My parents were taking me out for a family celebratory dinner after the graduation ceremony. I was just hoping we weren't going to the Sheraton.

Commencement was hard to take. Our names were called, and we were cheered on by our families and shouted at by our friends. We received our diplomas and a handshake from the principal and returned to our seats. We sang our class song; shifted our tassels; threw our mortarboards and that was it. Afterward, there were a lot of tears, hugs and high-fives. Party invites were delivered by word of mouth and everyone was doing something.

This was the end of our lives as we knew them, and everybody wanted to have one last bash before we said goodbye. Promises were made to try to get to each and every shindig, but that was damn near impossible.

One of Celia's friends cried hard on her shoulder and begged her to come to some 'girl's rager.' She was so weepy and pleading, I was afraid I was going to lose Celia for the night. Then I thought we could put our rendezvous on hold for another time, but Celia quelled that thought. She looked my way, winked at me and mouthed that it was all taken care of. *Thank God.*

Dinner with my family started out wonderful. We ate well and talked about a variety of subjects. My dad seemed to be warming to the idea of my attending college, even though he expressed his wishes that I'd picked 'a better field of study.'

"Is being an artist really going to land you a job?" My dad asked.

"Sure. There are a lot of jobs in the arts," I said. "Besides, I'm doing commercial art. I'll be doing advertising design; coming up with stuff for cereal boxes and improving labels on soup cans."

"I guess it sounds a little better when you put it that way," my dad said.

My mom asked about Celia and her plans, indicating she never talks about anything like work, or school.

"Actually, she's talked about a lot of things that she'd like to do," I said. "But never had anything definite in mind yet."

"She has to want to do something," my mom said.

"Well, her parents are a bit old-fashioned. They probably see Celia flourishing in the career of homemaker---wife and mother extraordinaire."

What I meant to say was: besides her folks being old-fashioned they weren't as pushy about careers and finding one's place in the world. I kept that to myself.

"They don't plan on marrying her off right away, I hope," my mom said, somewhat bitterly.

"No, not if I can help it," I responded. I could feel a nervous sweat beginning to bead.

My mom asked about 'our' plans for the future, and again I wasn't sure what to say. This was where our nice dinner conversation began to turn sour.

"We haven't talked much about it," I said. "We're planning to stay together, that much I do know."

"Well, that's nice!" My mom said, with a smile.

"I love her a lot. She's the best thing that's ever happened to me."

My dad furrowed his brow. "That's a bold statement," he said. "You two are so young."

"Not too young to know how we feel," I replied.

"You're too young to know she's 'the best thing that's ever happened' to you."

"But I *do* know. I've dated enough girls to have some idea."

"Celia hasn't dated much, though," my mom noted.

"She went out with a couple of guys before we met," I said. "But they didn't last. I'm the guy she's been with the longest."

"Longevity is good, I'll give you that," my dad stated. "But longevity at eighteen is a lot different than longevity at twenty-four or twenty-five."

"Why does age matter in this?" I asked.

"Because you're eight-*TEEN*," my dad said. "You graduated from high school an hour ago. You haven't even begun to live your life yet---you've got so much ahead of you."

I was getting frustrated. I wanted to leave, pick up Celia, skip the sleep over and just elope with her and shut everyone up for good. However, the conversation continued, and I was trying my best not to say something I would regret.

"I understand what you're saying dad," I said. "But how is it I'm not old enough to know I'm in love, but I *AM* old enough to buy cigarettes, vote and, well---join the military and get my head blown off in a war?"

"My God! You're not smoking, are you?!" My mom interjected in a panic.

"No. I'm not smoking," I assured her.

"Oh, thank Heaven for that."

The talk switched back to my dad and me.

"You're missing my point," my dad explained. "It's not all about age; it's about *experience*, and not settling on the first thing that comes along---or 'feels good.'"

"So, I'm supposed to keep looking?" I asked.

"It's not a bad idea."

"It is if I keep looking and it turns out Celia was the one all along."

"Well, then you'll *know* it's right."

"Not if I bail; realize she was the one and lose her altogether. That might be gaining 'experience,' but it's a bad lesson. I'd rather do what I'm doing and if I fail---it's on me."

"It's also on you if you do something stupid like run off and marry this girl on a whim, with no prospects and no future. That'll hurt the both of you and you will end up hating each other and..." my dad paused to collect his thought. "I guess, what I'm trying to say is that sometimes we *think* we know, but as we learn, we realize we had it wrong."

I wanted to cut my dad off and confess outright. I wanted to yell: "We're engaged!" But I did not.

"We'll just see how things go," I said. "I'm going to be leaving for school very soon and who knows what'll happen. Maybe Celia won't want to wait for me. I don't want to think like that, but hey..."

"Son, this is a tough time," my dad said. "You've got a great gal, but your life is just starting. You just need to let fate play her hand. Young love is the blindest kind."

After dinner, I shook my dad's hand and gave him a hug. I thanked him for the 'heart-to-heart,' even though he knew I wasn't going to fully heed his advice. My mom hugged me and gave me a kiss on my cheek and told me how proud she was of me and all that I'd done.

"My boy's grown up," she said, with an uneasy smile.

"I've still got a lot to learn," I said.

"We all do," she said. "Now go have some fun tonight with your friends. Your dad and I will see you tomorrow. Don't get into too much trouble!" She pushed me softly while tears welled in her eyes.

"I'll be good, I promise," I said.

I watched my folks get in their car and drive away. I waited until they were well out of sight before I got in my car to go and pick up Celia. My night was about to begin. I was so ready to see my love.

I thought about the conversation with my dad and as much as it pissed me off, he had some valid points, *but I did, too.* I knew my love for Celia was stronger than anything and after tonight we could let the world know we were no longer a couple, but *one.* I also thought about what my mom had said about not getting 'into too much trouble,' I was going to be safe and uphold my promise to *be good*---that promise also applied to Celia.

I drove to a little shop down the street from the restaurant. I picked up a six pack of ginger ale, a small box of condoms and tried my luck at buying a bottle of wine. I had no idea what I was doing. I grabbed a bottle of Cabernet Sauvignon. It was dark, red and sounded romantic and fancy. I placed the items on the counter and the clerk rang me up without batting an eyelash or asking for I.D. Wow! I felt like an absolute renegade.

CHAPTER 9

I picked Celia up at our friend Sarah's house---the same place I would drop her off tomorrow morning. We'd arranged this so as not to arouse suspicions. It was like something out of a movie: pure *Romeo and Juliet* stuff, but no light from windows breaking, or climbing down trellises or anything. It seemed so easy yet felt so sneaky. Only Sarah knew what was going on and swore an oath of secrecy.

I stopped across the street from the house and waited.

Celia walked out the front door, tote bag in hand like it was nothing.

"Did anyone see you?" I asked.

"No, her folks aren't home and there's a bunch of people here," Celia said. "It's a weird party, but a couple of girls are sleeping over after."

"This was perfect!"

"Yeah, I know! We couldn't have planned this any..."

Before she could continue, I grabbed Celia and pulled her to me. I kissed her hard as I gently held her face. We twisted and twirled passionately beneath the sporadically blinking, orange cone of a streetlight. It had seemed like an eternity since we'd been together, and I couldn't resist her once she was within my reach.

She pulled back dizzily. "Oh my, God! *Hello!*" She said, patting her chest and fanning her face.

"I've missed you," I said.

"I would never have known!" She responded.

"It's been too long."

"It's only been a couple of days."

"A couple of very, very long days."

"A couple of very, *very* long days," Celia replied, with a nod.

"Let's not prolong them anymore, OK?" I said, as I pointed to the car.

I opened the door and helped Celia into the car. I placed her tote bag into the backseat.

She looked up at me, lovingly, but so innocent through the open window. I smiled back at her. All I could feel was love---everything that coursed within my body felt like what I'd imagined bliss and rapture to feel like.

I got in the car and could smell Celia's perfume. *Chantilly* was her scent and the fragrance filled my car and sent my senses reeling.

"Are you ready to go, my love?" I asked.

"Yes. Ready to go---with you to Heaven and beyond," she replied.

We drove slowly down the street and headed out of town. I wasn't sure where we were going; I just knew it would be some-place away from familiar people and surroundings. I knew it would have a bed with clean linens and a bathtub and TV. Even though it may not be perfect, for us, tonight---it would be Para-dise.

The farther we moved from town, the darker it got as we headed away from the buzz and cold glow of the streetlight-s; lamp-lit homes and the multi-colored glare and drone of the neon signs of businesses, bars and the local bus station.

We'd had a quiet drive so far. What was there to say? *Plenty, I know,* but in every sense, we were heading into the un-known and that made conversation difficult to muster.

"How was dinner with your folks?" Celia asked out of the blue.

I was caught off guard by the question. "Yeah. It was al-right," I said haphazardly.

"Um... OK...?" she said.

"Sorry. I was just... Dinner was pretty good," I said.

"Nice."

"My dad and I had an interesting chat."

"Really? What about?"

"Just..." I paused. "...life and stuff. You know my dad, and how he's not sure what to make of me going to school for art and all. He doesn't think it's a good 'career path.'"

Celia chuckled and said, "Yeah, your dad is a straight-forward guy. He's not..."

"Abstract?" I asked, interrupting her.

"Yes! That's it," Celia said. "He's not 'abstract.'"

"No, he's not. That was pretty much what we talked about."

"Not the best dinner conversation, though?"

"It was *enlightening* I have to say that. I'm sure he'll come around someday. Perhaps I'll design a logo or an ad for a new sports car or power tool, then dad can say 'I knew that boy would do something great!' He can brag to everyone about me. He'd make both of us proud!" I said beaming.

Celia smiled and nodded. "Your parents are so different from mine," she said.

"Ain't that the truth," I said.

From here we returned to being quiet. The inside of the car was aglow with the lights of the dashboard on our faces; permeated with the sweet smell of Celia's perfume and rife with an uncomfortable silence.

We continued driving. We still hadn't found *our place* yet and it was getting later and later. We were on the freeway and it seemed like we were on the run; driving faster and with an uncertain sense of abandon and carelessness. It was stimulating.

As we ventured, we crossed between the new freeway and the old one. Signs posted indicated all the improvements: *a new and better way to get from here to there.* It seemed like a good thing, this unencumbered route. You could feel the difference in time between the old and new roads as the pavement changed; concrete to asphalt and back again. It was a sign of the times. We were moving toward the future and you either had to keep up or get left behind. It was exhilarating---and frighten-ing---to think about.

I rolled down the window to hear the night sounds and the changing tones of the road beneath the car. Celia followed suit and I kept glancing at her, watching the wind blow her hair back; seeing her slowly and dreamily toss her head from side-to-side.

We drove past a sign that caught my attention. At one time, I'm sure it was prominently displayed, but with the com-ing of the new freeway, was no longer viable; paint chipping away, fading and becoming overgrown with foliage. It was a sign for a motel. It had a cute, cartoonish painting of a swan and its cygnets. I spied the motel's slogan:

Just Ahead---On 27! Downy Pillows and a
Slice of Heaven---Come on in!

I looked at Celia and spoke, "I've found it."

"What?" She asked.

"Where we're going to spend the night," I said.

We shifted off the new freeway and found ourselves on a dark road again. A soft glow began to appear behind the trees along the roadside and we passed a haggard, rusty sign for south-bound U.S 27.

"This seems weird," Celia said.

I began to feel the same way until we came around a bend and saw the motel. It was an adorable place: an old bungalow type like you'd find in a classic road movie. When Celia saw the animated sign and read the name of the place she was smitten.

"*The Sleepy Swan Inn.* Oh my God, this is so great!" She shouted, clapping and smiling like a giddy schoolgirl.

This *was* the perfect place. The more I thought about it, the more I realized how well it fit Celia. We could make love at the Ritz Carlton, amid the most posh and modern amenities and it wouldn't be right. No. *This* was it: delicate, understated and old-fashioned; yet pleasing, comforting and beautiful. It had a quiet grace, but a bold charm; quirky and fun, but innocent and honorable---just like Celia. A huge, flickering neon VACANCY sign welcomed us.

The window to the office was illuminated by a dim, fuzzy ball behind a curtain. It looked more like a ghost than a light. Celia and I opened the door and a little bell chimed above our heads.

"That's so cute," Celia said, looking around the office.

The office had a large desk and a wall of mail slots behind it. A few of the slots had papers stuffed into them, others were empty, some had keys.

A tarnished, silver call bell sat on the edge of the desk. The innkeeper was nowhere to be found and it just made the whole scenario too classic.

"I want to ring the bell," Celia whispered.

"I think we have to," I said.

Celia tapped on the ringer and the bell clanked dully with each strike. It sounded sad. We both covered our mouths and quietly giggled at the ring---or lack thereof.

We heard a chair slide across a wooden floor and then the sound of footsteps. A long, fat shadow was thrown across the side wall and when we saw the innkeeper, we were surprised to see that such a mighty shadow had been cast by this tiny, old woman.

She had a happy beam about her face and a smile of someone who'd just been reunited with her lost children.

"Oh, my goodness! Just look at you two!" The innkeeper said, putting on a pair of glasses and cinching her sweater. "Welcome to the Sleepy Swan, will you be needing a room?"

"Yes ma'am," I responded.

"Well, alright! Will you be staying for the night or be needing the room for longer? We have weekly rates, too."

"We'll just be staying the night."

"Will you be needing a twin room, queen size, or a king?"

I looked at Celia. She smiled and beamed. I had my answer.

"Can we get a king, please?" I asked.

"Yep, we've got a couple available. Would you like an icebox in your room? It'll be a dollar extra," the innkeeper stated.

"Yes, we'd like an icebox," I said.

The innkeeper wrote, looked up and smiled at Celia.

"You're as cute as a button, honey," she said. "Most beautiful skin I've ever seen. So clean and smooth---ah, I used to be a doll like you, but that was so long ago," she said as she went back to writing.

Celia blushed. She thanked the innkeeper for her kind words.

I looked at Celia and confirmed the innkeeper's accolades, "See? I'm not the only one who thinks you're beautiful."

Celia blushed even harder.

The innkeeper gave us our keys. They hung on beaded chains from faded, plastic key tags. The numbers had been worn off long ago. She also gave us a piece of paper with a hand-written menu on it. There wasn't much to choose from: doughnuts, Danishes and coffee cakes to eat; coffee, orange, grape or apple juice to drink---all breakfast items and undoubtedly 'catered' from a store nearby. Nevertheless, it fit with the cute motif.

"Your room number is forty-six," the innkeeper said, "It's hard to read them tags," she added. "The menu doesn't say what time breakfast is, but if you get here before nine o'clock, there's usually a few goodies left. Pretty tasty stuff, too, so you gotta' get here!"

I smiled. "We'll try our best to get here early," I said.

Celia nodded and said, "We'll probably be hungry in the morning."

"I'm pretty sure we will be," I added, with a sly grin.

The innkeeper pointed us in the direction of our room and bid us a good night. She had to know exactly what we were going to do in that room; I'm sure she'd seen a million couples just like us pass through that office and take up in those rooms over the years. I had to imagine that not a whole lot of *sleeping* went on at the Sleepy Swan Inn.

We moved the car and parked directly in front of our room. Celia got out and went to unlock the door. As she did, I pulled my purchases from behind the seat.

"What's that?" she asked, her head tilted curiously.

"Just a couple things I bought for the evening," I said.

"Really? What did you get?"

"A couple surprises. Things we may need. Stuff like that."

I pulled the wine bottle out of the bag to show Celia a hint of it.

"It's why I paid the extra buck for the room," I said.

Celia waited for me to join her in the doorway before entering the room and turning on the light.

"I want us to share the first look," she said.

We stepped in almost simultaneously and Celia hit the light switch. Two large glass-ball lamps with tall woven shades weakly lit the room. The dull glow from behind the thick shades looked orange, however, the bulbs beamed brightly out the top and bottom of the shades, creating rays that cast strong spotlights on the ceiling and the nightstands upon which the lamps were placed.

We looked around the room and were so taken by what we saw. This room was like stepping back in time. The walls were wood paneled, and the floor was covered in orange shag carpet. The vibrant floral patterns of the bedspread matched almost perfectly with the upholstery in the room. The red, white, purple and orange colors made it feel like you could set a pizza down on the bed, couch or desk chair and never find it. It looked like something out of a bad 1960s TV show: kitschy, outdated, homely---and absolutely wonderful.

Celia ran and jumped onto the massive king-sized bed and it dwarfed her.

"Oh my God! This place is so..." she paused.

"Perfect?" I mused.

"Yes! It *is* perfect!" Celia said, with a slight squeal of delight.

I loved the TV. There was no remote control and it was on an old, wooden roller cart. I pulled the on/off switch and waited for the tubes to warm up and picture to fade in. The picture was bad, so I adjusted the rabbit-ear antennas to try and clear it up. It was no good. The picture was just bad and that was OK with us. I flipped the dial until I found something clear.

"Will this be alright to watch?" I asked.

"I'd rather listen to the radio, if that's OK," Celia said.

"Sure. That'll be fine."

I turned on the little desk radio and found a station that was playing decent music. I put the wine and ginger ale into the refrigerator to keep it chilled.

I popped the bathroom light on and had a look. The tub was an old, cast-iron, claw foot design and looked like it was brand new. The white paint was pristine and gleaming. The chrome fixtures were ancient but were highly polished and absolutely beautiful. The innkeeper and her staff kept this place in tip-top shape, that's for sure. I can't help but wonder if when the new freeway is completed this wonderful, little gem from the past will be able to stand up to the onslaught of the future's progress?

Celia patted the mattress and invited me to join her on the bed. I didn't have to be told twice. I sat down on the edge, kicked my shoes off and pulled myself alongside her. I put my head in her lap and stared up into her eyes. Her face was upside-down, and it looked weird to see her this way. I laughed.

"What's so funny, love?" She asked with a smile.

"Nothing," I said. "You're so beautiful---even upside-down."

I rolled over and sat up facing Celia. "Now, we're even," I said.

Celia giggled and asked me to kiss her. I put my hands on her cheeks, drew my face close to hers and we kissed. I pulled myself closer to her and could feel her arms wrapping tightly around me. The only sounds that could be heard in our room were our hastened breathing, and the soft smacking of our lips, whatever song was playing on the radio and the low, buzzing hum of the lamps and the refrigerator.

Celia fell back on the bed and pulled me down with her. I moved my hands slowly down her body; touching her through her clothes. I felt her open her legs and I pushed my groin tighter to hers. I had an erection and the harder I pushed against Celia, the stronger it became. She wrapped her legs around me.

I began to slowly thrust my hips, pushing my crotch harder to hers. I felt myself getting quite aroused as I continued dry-humping Celia. I didn't want to stop, but I did.

I pulled away. "I have to stop, just for a minute," I said.

"Are you OK?" Celia asked.

"Yeah. It's just that I'm..."

All of a sudden, a dull, but somewhat loud hum began emitting through the wall of our room right at the head of the bed. A couple of seconds later a steady rhythmic thumping began against the wall. My erection subsided quickly. I got freaked out not knowing what the hell was making these noises. I put my hand and ear to the wall trying to figure out the mystery.

"Aha!" I said.

I spied the small coin box on the side of the bed and knew right away what we were dealing with.

"What is it?" Celia asked.

"*That* is what it is," I said.

"*What?*"

I pointed to coin box. "*That*," I said. "This is a vibrating bed."

"Oh, wow," Celia said, slightly embarrassed. "But why was the vibrating bed next door making you stop?"

"It wasn't," I said. "But it was getting to that."

She was still confused.

"I was getting really excited," I said blushing. "I didn't want to go too far just yet."

"So, what would've happened?"

"Something I wasn't ready for. Let's put it this way: guys are a mess. We can't control ourselves."

"Why don't you let yourself lose control?"

I wanted this conversation to end. "It's just... I wasn't ready, that's all," I said, stuttering. "I want to be making love to you when it happens."

Celia smiled. "So, what does *it* feel like?" She asked.

"Which *it*?" I wondered aloud.

"*IT, it:* making love *it*. How does it make you feel?"

"It's impossible to explain. I know how it feels for me, but not for a girl."

"But you've had sex before---with a couple of girls, right."

"Yes."

"Did you ask them how it felt?

"No."

"Why not? Weren't you curious?"

"Maybe a little, but..."

Celia cut me off.

"Why didn't you ask them?" She posed. "Is it some 'guy thing'?"

"No. It's nothing like that. It's..." I said, unsure of what my next words would be.

"It's what?" Celia asked. Her face screwed up slightly.

"You want me to tell you the truth?" I asked. "Really?"

"Yeah, I do."

"I didn't love them. That's why I didn't ask. I didn't care."

I was bordering on anger---not at Celia, but at myself for being so uncaring and selfish about my past sexual encounters.

"Oh, my... I'm sorry..." Celia said, backing away from me.

"No, it's not like that," I said. "I did feel *something* for them, but I didn't know... I didn't bother to think about all of that."

Celia seemed to understand and posed a question for me that I had no choice but to answer.

"When we make love, are you going to wonder what it

feels like for me?" She asked.

"Yes. And I'll ask you with every movement, touch and stroke," I said without hesitation. "Because I truly love you and want to know how I make you feel all over."

Celia said nothing. She just sat on the bed and smiled. She'd won a personal victory. Her prize was that she got to tell me how it felt for her. However, with Celia being a virgin, I'm not sure if she actually knew what her expectations were, or if she was going to like what she felt.

Our conversation had created an unexpected tension between us. I was scared that I'd ruined not just another night, but *a night of all nights* thanks to my stupidity. We sat silent. *Why do I always do this?*

The bed next door started up again. Celia and I laughed loudly. We fell into each other's arms and began kissing amid the hum and thump of our neighbor's massage. Any bad vibes that loomed were now gone.

"Maybe we should try ours," Celia suggested. "We could have a competition!"

"They may have a head start," I said. "But I'll bet we could win!"

CHAPTER 10

We'd been at the Sleepy Swan for over three hours and in that time, we'd made out, laughed at our neighbors and had a small tussle that turned out to be nothing. We'd come here to make love but were still dressed and Celia was still a virgin. It felt like it was so late, but it wasn't quite midnight. Our night together was patchy---not bad, but typical.

I began to recall my first time and what a harrowing mess it was: bad movie, bad restaurant and a bad car. We ended up sweaty and oblivious in the backseat of the aforementioned bad car.

We'd parked on an abandoned airfield. The night was warm, and the sky was dark; starless and cloudy. Everything around us seemed rife with the noise of crickets and dotted with the glow of fireflies.

We were both virgins. I came within a minute of entering her, but she had no idea. I hid my embarrassment by moving around a lot. She was in pain the whole time, but never said a word. She bled all over the backseat of the car. I was wearing a condom, but it had a hole in it. We freaked out, but then thought---like so many others before us---*nothing can happen the first time.* She apologized the whole drive home---both for bleeding and not telling me it hurt. I apologized for carrying a condom in my wallet for so long.

Over the next several weeks we lived in fear that she'd gotten pregnant. She did not. We chalked our luck up to the belief about nothing happening the first time.

My second time wasn't much better: decent restaurant, no movie and nearly coming to blows with a carny at the fair over a stuffed dragon that I'd clearly won.

The topper was another case of premature ejaculation---even more embarrassing this time. Again, I tried to hide it by moving around, although I think she knew by my expression it had happened. A little of this and a little of that and we were on again. It seemed to take me two times to get things right. I was hoping to God that tonight with Celia a *warning shot* would not be fired.

I moved off the bed and walked to the refrigerator. Celia asked what I'd bought. I pulled out the six pack of ginger ale and set it on the table. Next, I took out the bottle of wine. Celia got a funny look on her face I'd never seen before. I wasn't sure what to make of it.

"What's wrong?" I asked.

"Better question for you is: what's *that?*" Celia posed.

"I showed it to you before. It's wine. It's for us. Something to help us get us in the mood."

Celia's expression remained the same. "I've never had wine before," she said.

"I have. It's not bad," I said. "I bought this one, because I couldn't pronounce it. If you can't pronounce it, it's supposed to be *even* better." I smiled and pointed at the label.

"*Cab*... what the...? How *do* you pronounce that?" Celia asked, intently studying the label.

"Well, it's French," I said. "So, I'm assuming you don't pronounce the last letters of the words: Caber-*nay* Saw-ving-*YONG*... I think. I have no idea."

Celia seemed impressed with my tackling of the name and overdone French accent.

"Ooh! How romantic!" She said. "*Oui, oui!* That's about all the French I know."

"I'm sure you know more," I said. "You remember the names of the stuff we had for dinner at the hotel, right? That's French."

"Oh yeah! I feel culturally enriched," she said. "So *international.*"

I laughed as I searched for a couple of glasses to drink from. As I looked around the room, I began peeling the foil cover from the top of the bottle. I found drinking vessels, while simultaneously discovering I was going to need a corkscrew. *Damn it.*

Celia noticed I was struggling with something and asked what was wrong.

"It would seem I need a corkscrew to open this wine," I said in a huff.

"Can't you use something else?" She asked.

I thought about it. "Yeah, let me go get a screwdriver out of the car," I said. "That should work."

"Glad I could help," Celia said

"Me, too!" I said, as I kissed her and walked out to the car.

I returned with a Phillips-head screwdriver and a determined look on my face. I set the bottle down hard atop the table. I presented the screwdriver to Celia like a hand model displaying a product in a commercial. She smiled and pulled herself up on the bed; this was quite a show I was about to put on---she didn't want to miss it.

I held the neck of the bottle and twisted the screwdriver into the top of the cork. I pushed it down and tried to pry it out. No go. I shoved the screwdriver hard into the cork and pushed it down until it dropped into the bottle. Little bits of cork flew as I yanked the screwdriver from the out of the bottle.

"Impressive," Celia said, with a hint of sarcasm.

"Control yourself, woman," I said in a bad cowboy voice.

I poured Celia's glass first, then mine.

"Careful of any cork bits," I said. "And if it tastes a bit like my screwdriver, I apologize."

We touched glasses and said 'cheers' to each other. I took the first sip and it wasn't bad. Celia, however seemed less than impressed with the flavor.

"It tastes like really strong grape juice and wood," she said.

"That's the age and fermentation thing," I stated, trying

to sound knowledgeable.

"Maybe the more I drink the better it will taste?"

"Yeah, that's kinda' the way alcohol seems to work."

It had been awhile since we'd both eaten, so it wasn't taking long for the wine to affect us. I poured another glass and gave myself a little bit more this time. Celia was still working on her first go-around and was having a difficult time with it.

"I want to like this, but it just isn't good," she said apologetically.

I got her a ginger ale from the refrigerator. "Here, my love," I said. "Sip the wine; then chase it with this."

"Can I pour the soda into the wine?"

"I don't see why not. It'll be like a freaky wine cooler."

Celia poured a goodly amount of ginger ale into her wine; the Cabernet Sauvignon changed colors from dark red to magenta. She took a sip and said it was better.

We drank and talked a bit in between glasses. The whole idea was to make things go a little easier; to loosen us both up and let our inhibitions down. The more I drank; the more ready I was to make love to Celia. She was running a few cups behind, but I knew she was feeling the effects as well. I poured myself another cup and offered Celia some more. She passed but said she would have more later.

"How do you feel?" I asked.

"Weird... but weird *good*," she said. "It's kinda' nice."

I drew close to her and we kissed. There's something about intoxicated kissing that amps it up a little. We weren't drunk but were on our way. I felt warm and very amorous; my penis going from indifferent to half-erect.

Celia was very hands-on, touching and feeling more than usual. It seemed our skin had become hypersensitive and every stroke of our hands were like a sending a shock through our systems.

"Would you like to play a little?" I asked seductively.

"What do you have in mind?" Celia wondered aloud.

"I've got a game I'd like to try. It's like strip *Truth or*

Dare," I said. "We ask each other questions. If you can't or won't answer, you have to take off an article of clothing. If you do answer, the person who asked the question has to take something off. Sound fun?"

Celia furrowed her brow. "It does sound fun," she said. "But very weird and very... *guy.* OK. I'll play."

I offered to go first. I tried to think of a question that would strip Celia in one fell swoop, but I couldn't. I wanted to win on the first try; however, I started off with something simple.

"Have you ever stolen anything?" I asked.

"Yeah, I stole a pack of gum from the local five-and-ten when I was thirteen," Celia answered without hesitation.

I was surprised. "Really?" I asked. "Wow!"

I took off both of my socks.

It was Celia's turn. "Have *you* ever stolen anything?" She asked. "It has to beat a pack of gum."

I thought about it. "Yes. I hoofed a pack of cigarettes from my grandma," I said proudly. "My cousins and I smoked the whole pack."

"That's a winner!" Celia said, as she took off her watch.

"No fair!" I cried. "A pack of smokes totally trumps a pack of gum any day---especially stolen from your grandmother. Lose something else."

Celia took off her shoes.

"Three things for that," she said.

"Where'd you get 'three'?" I asked.

"One watch---and two shoes."

"OK. Yeah, so three *paltry* things. I was hoping for a blouse."

I poured us some more wine. I was starting to loosen up; Celia was farther along with even less. We were looking at each other in the most overtly sexual ways but had yet to relent to our desires. We played on.

It was my turn again and I wanted to pull out all the stops. By now we were both half-dressed and I needed the win. I was feeling very male. Celia was not supposed to win this game. She would lay naked and vulnerable on the bed before I'd shed another stitch of clothing---or so I thought.

"What is the stupidest... no wait... most *unYOU* thing you've ever done?" I asked, thinking I had this.

"I got high with my sister's boyfriend," Celia proclaimed almost boastfully.

I was blown away. "You win," I said, as I stripped off the rest of my clothes leaving me in just my underwear.

"What?!" Celia asked.

"You got high. I didn't see that coming. You win!"

"No way. *You've* never gotten high?"

I was flabbergasted. "Uh, *yeah*... I have... but you're not... really? You did?!" I said, rambling.

"It was only once," Celia confirmed.

I sat on the bed, just my briefs between the linens, Celia and what God gave me. I was so floored. *My* Celia would never smoke grass, let alone do it with someone she wasn't close to. I needed answers.

"So... Patty's boyfriend... and..." I stammered, dumbfounded.

"Yeah, I went with Patty to his house one time," she said. "He passed around a pipe and..."

"You hit it?"

"I did. I felt so stupid afterward, but I just had to... just to say I did."

I smiled uncomfortably. "How'd you... what did you think?" I asked.

"It was weird. OK, but weird," Celia said, not giving away too much.

I found her lack of being forthcoming a bit intimidating. I'd smoked dope, but now feared that my innocent, naïve and uncorrupted fiancée had smoked better stuff than I had. In some alternate, backward dimension this worked, but in *this* world---it did not.

"You lie!" I said, half-joking.

"No, I really did," she said matter-of-factly.

"You think you know a person."

"What?"

"Nothing. It's just hard to imagine you doing anything like that."

"You still love me, though, right?"

"Of course! Don't be silly. Now I'm curious about other things you've done---besides being a dope-smoking gum thief," I said with a smile.

Celia looked as if she was hurt by my assessment of her behavior. I meant no harm.

"I'm sorry," I said woefully. "That was stupid of me to say."

"It's OK," she responded.

I did what any dumb ass would do after saying something foolish to their true love: I poured us another glass of wine.

"Here. A peace offering," I said sheepishly.

"Do we really need more?" Celia wondered.

"Sure. It makes things better."

Celia added some ginger ale to her wine making another crimson panache. She sipped and smiled from her cup. I watched her eyes sparkle. I wanted to take off my underwear. Celia peered down and noticed my bulge.

"Someone's happy," she said, gesturing to my crotch.

"Oh, geez!" I exclaimed, somewhat embarrassed. "You weren't supposed to see that---at least not yet."

"I like it. I like that I do that to you," she said. "Can I see it---*really* see it?"

I did not hesitate. I slipped off the bed, pulled my underwear down to my feet and stepped out of them. I stood naked before Celia. She covered her mouth and gasped. Her eyes sparkled again, and her pupils dilated as she stared at my sex: hard and lightly pulsing with my speeding heartbeat.

"I've never seen one before," Celia stated. "Well, not like this."

She looked at me and studied my body.

"It's not much to look at, really," I said, somewhat embarrassed by my perceived lack of size.

"No, it's... I didn't know what to expect," she said. Her timbre rang of astonishment.

"Guys always wish theirs were bigger."

"Uh, uh... I think it's plenty big. Big enough for me."

I blushed and bent in a little. I felt a bit self-conscious. For what it was worth, I was Celia's measuring stick. Her being with another could never happen; however, my size and my performance would be used to compare every experience from here on out. It was a lot to comprehend.

Celia looked at me and slowly pulled herself off the bed. She stepped to me and began kissing my neck. I could feel my erection getting even harder. Celia moved into me and the tip of my penis was rubbing all over the front of her pants.

I was getting crazy. I wanted to touch myself so badly, but my hands were full with Celia as I stroked her body, randomly trying to undo hooks and buttons; pushing fabric aside to access her better. I moved a bra strap aside and kissed her bare shoulder, while smelling her skin. I licked the groove of her clavicle and ran my tongue up her neck. She moaned softly. My mouth found its way to hers and we kissed hard and deep.

I pulled away from her mouth and kissed her neck again. Celia started talking in whispers and asked me something I couldn't understand.

"What, my love?" I asked, in a whispered pant.

She answered, "What are you thinking right now?"

I was on sensory overload and couldn't catch a single thought as they whizzed through my brain. I blurted out the first tangible thing I could grasp.

"The other night when we went out," I said. "I went home and masturbated."

That was my answer. Not how much I wanted to make love to her; not could she finish undressing; not even another question about the wine or a comment about her getting stoned. No. I told her I jerked off. *How romantic.*

Celia paused and oddly enough, laughed at my statement. "Really?" She asked.

I shook my head and apologized to her.

"I don't know where that came from," I said sounding stupid. "I'm just like…"

"It's OK. I wasn't expecting *that* for sure!" She replied.

Celia got a devilishly inquisitive look on her face---I knew what she was going to ask.

"What does it feel like when you do it?" She asked.

I didn't want to reveal anything. There are reasons we do it, yet for as much as masturbation is almost instinctual, even good for you---it is quite taboo. Guys are jerking off every second all over the world, but we're not supposed to talk about it. It's dirty. It's base. It's something we tease each other about. It is not something one brings up while on the fringe of making love, even though there is a direct correlation between the acts. Regardless of all this---I knew Celia wanted an answer.

"It feels really, *really* good," I proclaimed.

"You just do it?" Celia asked.

"Yeah, but not all the time. Just when you're feeling *pent up.*"

"Like when your true love won't sleep with you yet?"

"Kind of like that. There's other things, too."

"Like what?"

"Anything to do with porn; thinking about someone you have the hots for but could never be with. Sometimes you do it because you're bored. Other times you just have this weird craving and need to ejaculate. That's what it's all about: coming."

I was hoping I'd answered Celia's questions and quelled her curiosities about why boys can't keep their hands to themselves, but I knew she had more to ask.

"So, what do *you* think about when you do it?" She wondered.

"I don't know. Just *stuff,* I guess," I said as honestly as possible.

"What kind of 'stuff'? There has to be something. I mean, I didn't even know you did that."

"It's not something you talk about publicly. It's really filthy when you get down to it."

"I'm curious now. How long have you done it?"

I cringed. "Since I was in fifth grade, I think," I said.

"Oh my!" Celia said with a gasp.

"Yep. That's my legacy, I suppose."

"You still didn't answer my question, though. What do *you* think about when you do it?"

I wanted to give Celia a solid answer so that she would be satisfied, and we could move on. I didn't want to discuss masturbation anymore, especially with her---it was just too awkward a subject. I thought about swearing off it completely after this. I tried to come up with something.

"I can't say anything without it sounding weird," I offered as my response.

"Do you think about old girlfriends?" Celia asked, with slight disgust.

"I have, but that was a while ago."

"Why would you think about an ex?"

"I don't know. It's probably because of what I'd said about not having something, or wanting to have done something nasty to them. I really don't know. Can we change the subject?"

"You're uncomfortable?"

"Yeah! That's putting it mildly. I love you and we're here to make love, not talk about *lonely boy private time*."

Celia giggled and agreed. However, she did have one last question.

"When you did it the other night after our date... did you think about me?" She asked.

I closed my eyes hard and shook my head. "No," I said.

"Why?"

"Because I love you."

"But shouldn't that be a reason to want to do it? You think about the one you love and how they make you feel and well..."

"That would be nice, but it's not the case."

"Why not?"

"Because jerking off is selfish. It's all about you and your desires. To pleasure yourself while thinking about the one you love makes the relationship feel cheap and sleazy. I don't want to think of you like that. I want to think of *us*---not just me."

Celia could tell I was frustrated. She'd put me on the spot. Usually I can work my way through her interrogations, but this one was tough. I was hoping to God we were done.

"I'm sorry if I've embarrassed you," she said, giving me a soft kiss on the cheek.

"It's OK. I just..." I said, uncertain.

"Can I make it up to you?"

"I suppose, but I'm not sure how."

"Here..."

CHAPTER 11

Celia softly pushed me toward the bed and hit my shoulders just hard enough to knock me back. I lay on the bed flat, my legs over the edge and my sex pointing straight at the ceiling.

She reached behind her back and unhooked her bra. She slinked out of the straps and pulled them down over her arms. She asked me to spread my legs, then bent down slightly and brought her chest to my crotch. She leaned in closer and pressed herself to me, squeezing my penis between her breasts.

I watched the head disappear and slowly re-emerge; up and down between her soft, petite tits. Celia moaned and pushed her breasts together harder and began to move faster. I'd never had this done to me before. It felt great. After several minutes, I could feel myself getting close to orgasm.

"Celia, I'm going to come," I said. She didn't stop.

"Oh my God, you have to stop, or I'm going to come on you."

She kept going. She was pumping me between her tits even harder now and I could feel my body on the verge of ejaculation. If she didn't stop, I was going to make a mess all over her chest, neck and face. I tried to move away. I tried to hold it back, but I couldn't. I was in orgasm and about to climax. I sat up and pushed Celia away.

"What's wrong?!" She asked, sounding disappointed and angry.

"I don't want to do that," I said.

"What?"

"I don't want to come on you."

"Why not?! I want you to!"

"Why? Doesn't that seem kind of... nasty?"

"No. Not to me. It's from you.

"I want you to forget everyone and everything else you've ever done. I want to make new memories with you tonight. I want you to think about these things whenever you masturbate again. I want you to think about me and not feel selfish. I just want to please you."

I felt bad. When we decided to spend the night together, I figured there would be complexities, but not this kind.

I was definitely supposed to be forgetting 'everyone and everything else.' I had to let things happen. Celia wanted to make my dreams come true just as much as I wanted to make her first sexual experience one that she would lovingly remember. I needed to lighten up and let myself go---God knows Celia certainly had.

"I want to try again. Can we please? I won't stop you this time," I said.

Celia slowly swung her head in a circle. She put her hands on my thighs and stared intently at me. I figured she was going to work me again with her breasts, but that didn't happen.

"No. You had your chance," she said. "I don't know what to do with you."

The tone in her voice had me a little worried. I wasn't sure what to make of it and I figured---like so many times before---that our night was over.

"Sing to me," Celia demanded seductively. "You know what I want to hear."

"Ballad again?" I asked.

"Yes. Make it really torchy and beautiful. Make me feel it all over."

I wasn't sure how I was going to do this. The last time I'd sang 'Respect' as a ballad, it melted her, but this time I needed to put something else into it. She wanted to wear it like a silk robe, and I figured I owed it to her to do just as she asked. I thought about Edith Piaf and Billie Holiday and hoped I could channel their torchy, melancholy style.

I started singing slowly and throaty. Celia smiled and lay on the bed next to me. As I progressed through each verse, she kissed me, moving over my neck; down my chest and to my belly---I knew where she was going---I just couldn't believe it. *Was she really going to do this? Was she really going to suck me off?* I wasn't sure what to make of it all. My Celia, my innocent, little flower was about to put me into her mouth---giving me a blow-job seemed like the last thing she would ever do.

"Why did you stop singing?" Celia asked, looking at my penis and softly running her fingers over the shaft.

"Because I can't concentrate," I said.

"You don't have to," she said. "I want to do this. I want to taste you."

My heart began pounding in a cross between the nerves I'd already been experiencing and a new sensual excitement. It's been said that the penis doesn't truly 'throb.' The throbbing of the male member was a myth created by writers of romance and erotica to enhance a scene. Well, at this moment mine *was* throbbing. It was throbbing with my elevated heartbeat. It was throbbing like I'd just ejaculated, even though I hadn't yet.

"Where do you want me to start?" Celia asked. "You've seen *those* movies, so you probably know something about how to get going." She slowly ran her tongue along the bottom of my shaft: from the base of my scrotum to my head.

"Um… that was a good start," I said, taking a deep breath.

Suddenly, I felt wet. I felt surrounded by a warm, damp, softness. I was in Celia's mouth and she was gently sucking me. I was getting head and it felt amazing. She stopped.

"What?! Why did you stop?!" I asked, panicked.

"Has anyone done this to you before?" She asked. "Who was she?"

I was taken aback. Celia knew I'd had sex and that didn't faze her, but this seemed to be something else. Now, she wanted a name. I didn't want to answer. For a second I thought I'd lie and say she was the first, but sexual pleasure is like God's truth serum---I had to confess.

"Meredith," I said. "It was a girl named Meredith---only once, though."

"What a hussy. Meredith is a tramp," Celia stated, shaking her head.

"I couldn't lie to you," I said. "I want us to be completely honest with each other---even about this stuff."

Celia agreed. "This is the stuff we *should* be honest about. Thank you for telling me."

Her eyes rolled back in her head as she took me into her mouth again. She moved her head and my penis spun around the inside of her cheeks. She worked her tongue and I was in absolute ecstasy. Occasionally, her teeth would hit my skin. If I winced, she'd apologize. It sounded strange to hear her talk with her mouth full.

Celia pressed her face to my pubic hair. I was fascinated watching her take me so far into her throat. She pulled up and her lips tightened around the base of my head. This was pain-ful---but it was the best pain I'd ever felt.

"You can't do that," I said in a panting whisper.

She stopped and looked up at me. "Why not? Don't you like it?" She asked.

"Yeah, but it's a strange sensation---between pleasure and pain and... just do it a little *gentler,* OK?"

"Anything for my guy," Celia said, as she went back to work on me.

I put my hand on the back of her head and started pulling on her hair a little; guiding her as she drew in and drew out every inch of me. I was so amazed at how well Celia could give head. She made a few moves that definitely solidified this was her first time, but I think her inexperience made the sensation---and the act so much more incredible.

I could feel myself getting ready to come and I didn't want her to stop. I wanted this feeling to continue. I thought about holding her head down tighter, but she'd know I was up to no good. I thought about not telling her when I was about to come and just let it happen. The worst things she could do would be gag and spit it out, I thought. *Or be absolutely livid with me.* She wouldn't swallow it---there was no way. I started feeling guilty about it and told her I was about to come.

She didn't stop. I told her again. She kept going---faster now and a bit more forceful. It hurt and I wanted her to stop, or slow down.

"Celia... honey... I'm going..." I stammered.

She drew me out and moved her head, just as I ejaculated. I sat up as I came. My semen shot out like a lightning bolt. It was thick, pearlescent and smelled of bleach. What didn't get on the bed dropped into my pubic hair and onto my leg.

"Oh my God!" Celia cried. "Did I do that to you?!"

"Yes. Yes, you did my love," I said.

"That has to feel amazing."

"Oh, it does," I said, panting; trying to catch my breath. "It's the orgasm, the climax---the *everything*---all of these are what make sex feel so indescribable."

Celia gave me a moment to collect myself.

"What's the difference between sex and making love?" She asked.

"That's a debate," I said. "I think it's what you put into it and how you feel about the person you're with that differentiates them."

Celia stood up and took her pants off. I could see her panties were wet. She was ready for me to enter her body.

I got up off the bed and kissed her gently on the mouth. I wanted her so bad but wanted to clean myself off first.

"I need a minute," I said. Celia nodded in soft concurrence.

In the bathroom, as I washed my groin and legs with warm, soapy water I said to myself, *this is about to happen.*

We'd taken so many giant steps tonight and the next logical one was to make love, so why was I feeling like I was on the cusp of changing my mind? *No. This cannot be happening---not now.*

I'd wanted this night for so long and it was Celia who had

always been hesitant and resistant. Now, she had *definitely* taken on the role of aggressor and for as much as I found it exciting---it was quite intimidating. Celia had just turned the tables on me.

She'd pried into my soul and asked me things I never thought she would---things I never thought I'd answer. She did things that had been off-limits before, elevating her own sensuality and willingness to fantastic heights. She had never seen a man's penis up close before tonight, yet she took mine into her mouth without question. She had changed. I knew it was for the better, but it still scared me. I tried to settle my brain. She had changed---and it was all for me.

I walked out of the bathroom and Celia had poured two more glasses of wine for us. She was lying on the bed with her upper body propped by her elbows.

"You look presentable now, my dirty man," she said, lifting herself up.

"I don't feel as sticky; that's something," I said, with a laugh.

She took a big sip from her glass and set it on the nightstand. She handed me my glass when she'd finished.

"Drink my love," she said. "To us. To tonight. To forever."

"First and last and always, my darling," I said. I drained the entire glass in one swallow.

I got on the bed next to Celia and we spun about in a slow chase. I lightly tackled her, and we kissed again. I rubbed my sex against the wet fabric of her panties.

I moved quickly and got up. I grabbed Celia's underwear and pulled them to her ankles. She kicked them off onto the floor and there we were: completely naked. I'd seen her half-dressed before, but never like this---and it was worth the wait. Her pubic hair was thick and dark brown; her labia looked swollen and I could see her pink lips peeking from the tight curls of fur between her legs.

Celia looked at me and I returned the gaze. I slid toward her and got as close as I could to entering her without actually doing it. I moved my body down, sliding my head across her chest and belly. My face was in her soft fur when she told me to stop.

"What are you doing?" She whispered in slight shock.

"I'd like to return the favor," I said, hinting at eating her out.

"No. Not now."

I was surprised. "Why not? It'll feel incredible, I promise," I said as I smelled her sex.

"No. Not now," she repeated.

"Please?"

Celia shook her head. I lay my face down on her belly and looked up at her. I wanted to pleasure her so much and didn't understand why she wouldn't let me.

"What's wrong?" I asked.

"I don't want that now," she said implicitly. "I want to save that for our wedding night---a special treat."

"So, you want to have sex---*the biggest of all big things*---but I can't go down on you?"

"That's right."

"I don't understand."

"You always talk about 'guy stuff,' how guys do this and that. Well, this is *girl stuff* and I'm not ready for that. I want to--- just not now."

"Fair enough."

I rolled over and grabbed a condom from the box. I asked Celia if she still wanted to *do it,* and she nodded sharply. I put the condom on and slinked over to her. I eased her down on to the mattress and kissed her. I had her wrists in my grip and gently pushed myself between her legs. She opened wider. We still kissed. I pulled away.

"Are you ready, my love?" I asked.

"Yes," she whispered.

CHAPTER 12

I grabbed my sex at the base and guided it between Celia's legs. At this moment, I felt massive. She; however, looked so small. She was wet, but I didn't know if it was enough. I was worried I was going to cause her great pain. I was very careful. The tip of the condom disappeared amid her labia, but I was still not inside of her.

Celia closed her eyes. "Sex me first; then make love to me," she said softly. "I want to find out what each one feels like."

I moved lightly in small circles outside of her. This opened her a little more. I didn't say a word before I slowly pushed myself into her. Celia gasped and breathed deep as I kept filling her. I went as far as I could go and was fully inside of her. Our bodies pushed together tightly---we were one.

Celia was gritting her teeth. She was in pain. I didn't move at first. I didn't want to ruin this.

"Are you OK, Celia?" I whispered.

"It... feels... so..." she stammered.

"Different?"

"Why does it hurt so much?"

"Because you're so tight."

"Maybe it's because you're so big and I'm so tight," she said half laughing, half crying.

"Do you want me to stop?" I asked.

Celia pulled up and looked me straight in the eye. "No. I want you to fuck me," she ordered. "Fuck me and make me your woman."

I was blown away by what she said. I just...

I began thrusting my hips slowly into her. I laid down

closer to her to feel her body and give her a sense of security. She was still gritting her teeth and breathing hard behind them. It sounded like she was angry and fighting through the pain.

"Oh..." she cried out.

I wanted to stop.

"Don't stop," she pled. "Keep going. Keep making love to me."

Celia was in pain the whole time and I felt terrible. I could feel I was going to come again. When I finally ejaculated, it felt so intense I thought it had burst through the condom. It hadn't. I swear, I'd never come like that in my life.

I slowly pulled out of her and she bled all over. The bedspread was soaked in blood, but it was hard to tell. It blended into the color palate and design on the material too well. Celia was scared. She didn't know she would bleed so much. I held her tight to me and we rocked gently.

"I love you so much, Celia," I said as I kissed her hair.

"I love you, too. I love you forever," she responded.

"It's like we're married now."

"I want to feel that way. I want to know that this is good and right."

"It is, my love. It is. It's your first time and the first time isn't always great."

"But I'm not a virgin anymore. I'm yours now. I'm your woman."

"You were before, but you *truly* are now. Can I do anything for you?"

"Make love to me again."

"Let's wait, OK? Rest for a minute and then we'll do it again."

Celia yawned and curled closer to me.

"I think I do need some sleep," she said. "You wore me out."

I laughed at her assessment. "It takes some getting used to," I said.

"Let's take a nap and then we'll try again in a couple of

hours," Celia suggested.

"We should probably clean ourselves up a bit," I said, with a slight yawn.

We went into the bathroom together and washed each other. It was something so simple, but it seemed so intimate and romantic.

I looked at the clock and it was approaching two AM.

We pulled the bedspread back and Celia had bled through to the top sheet. She was so embarrassed. I told her not to worry.

"That sweet old lady is going to know what we did here," she said, horrified.

"We can make it more interesting," I said. "We can say we murdered someone in the bed."

"No! That's awful! That's even worse. I feel terrible."

"Trust me, that lady has seen a bloody sheet or two in this place. It's OK. I'll put a towel down."

I put the towel on the bed and Celia snuggled up to me. Within minutes she was asleep; softly snoring and a bit fidgety. I held her tightly and fell asleep, too.

We slept longer than we'd planned. I was awoken by a noise outside our room. I looked at the dull glow of the old electric clock. It was five AM.

"Oh my God, honey---wake up. It's five," I said in a panicked whisper.

Celia opened her eyes a peered around blindly. She didn't seem worried about the time and said it was 'OK.' She started to go back to sleep.

"What time do you need to be back at Sarah's?" I asked.

"Not until eight or so," she said. "We have lots of time. It was grad night---we're all out late."

CHAPTER 13

I watched Celia settle her naked body into mine once more and go out again. I couldn't go back to sleep. I was worried about the two of us getting into trouble. I started thinking about us and what our lives were going to be like after today. We had made the ultimate commitment and Celia had given me the ultimate gift.

I thought about traditions. Celia's family was very traditional. We were already engaged, but I still hadn't asked her dad for 'her hand.' I hadn't forgotten about the importance of that, I just hadn't done it yet. I would do it today, and if not today, then definitely tomorrow.

I watched the curtains in the room begin to glow with the light of the brightening dawn. It was almost six. Celia was still sound asleep. I was still worried about everything.

I wanted to move, but didn't want to wake Celia, even though I would have to very soon. I softly stroked her skin and talked quietly to her.

"You're so beautiful," I said. "I don't deserve you."

She shifted a little and mumbled something unintelligible before nuzzling up to me again. Birds chirped outside our window and their chaotic, tweeting songs made me smile.

I went back to my earlier thoughts about how today would be. I'd been out of high school a little less than twelve hours and already so many things in my life had changed. I began to plan my day---trying to be an adult---trying to make a schedule. First thing was to get Celia back to Sarah's, then I would go home and do what I needed to do there. I'd call work and see if they wanted me today. Later, I'd go and buy Celia flowers and take them to her. I *would* talk to her dad today. I know I had a few other things to do, but I forgot them.

Celia rolled over and stretched. Her eyes were bleary and bloodshot. She peered around the room and looked lost. She pushed her hair from her face and looked down at herself and then at me. She quickly covered up. It was a subconscious move, one of modesty, as if she didn't know why she---and I---were naked.

"You forgot already?" I asked, shaking my head.

"No. I'm sorry," she said. "I don't usually wake up with no clothes on."

"Is it just the lack of clothes, or the lack of clothes and the fact that there's a nude dude in bed with you, as well?"

"Probably both---and it's not my bed, either."

We laughed and Celia put her head on my chest.

"Did you sleep at all?" She asked.

"A bit," I said. "But not as much as you, my love."

"I have to say: making love definitely makes you tired," she commented.

I kissed Celia's forehead and stroked her hair. We were lying together quietly and didn't want to get out of bed, but we had to. We were running short on time and still had to shower and check out of the motel.

"I'll shower first, then you, OK?" Celia said.

"Sure. That will be fine," I said.

Celia got out of bed and I watched her walk to the bathroom, her hips moving with the distinctly, feminine bounce that drives guys crazy. I whistled at her just as she turned and went through the bathroom door. She didn't respond at first, then leaned backward out of the door jamb.

"Why don't we save some water and time; come and take a shower with me," she said, motioning me to her with her hand.

I got out of bed to join her in the bathroom. When I came in, she was sitting on the toilet wiping herself.

"Sorry---bad timing?" I asked, slightly embarrassed.

"No, it's fine," she said. "I'm just still so bloody."

"I apologize for that as well."

Celia finished cleaning up and then we brushed our teeth together and started our shower. The tub was deep. I helped her over the lip. The water was perfect: warm and soothing.

Celia pulled the curtain around and began to wash. She stood with her back to the showerhead and the water poured through her hair. I'd never seen her like this before. Her face was more pronounced; the water darkened her hair, made her skin glow and accentuated her freckles. Her body was slick and slippery and gleamed; while the drops of water beaded on her face.

"Would you like to wash me?" Celia asked handing me the soap.

I moved toward her and began rubbing the soap slowly on her skin. I seemed to be focused on her belly, as that was the only place I was applying soap.

"I think that's clean, honey," she said. "There's lots of other dirty parts that need attention."

I lathered her body as she moved beneath the showerhead. She was covered in soap and little bubbles.

She took the soap from me and washed her face. While she was rinsing her face off, I lathered my hands with soap and stood behind her and began massaging her breasts. Celia was quiet as I gently squeezed them, pressing her nipples between my thumbs and forefingers until they'd become erect and hard.

"What are you doing to me?" She asked with a groan.

"Making you feel good and helping you get clean," I responded, as I kissed her shoulder and pushed my body against hers.

"Let's make love again," I whispered into the curve of her neck.

"We can't. You don't have a condom."

"I don't need one. The water is hot enough to kill my soldiers. You don't have to worry," I explained.

Celia turned around and slid her chest to mine. We kissed and I put my hand between her legs and softly rubbed.

"Oh my God! What are you doing?" She asked. A look of

shock and unexpected pleasure came across her face.

"I'm making sure you're ready."

"Oh my God. You didn't... why didn't I feel this last night?!"

"Because you wouldn't let me go down on you. I didn't get to play with your clit," I explained. "That's what makes *this* happen."

Celia put her left foot on the lip of the tub, opening herself wider. I rubbed her faster and she gasped. She grabbed me and pulled closer. She bumped her forehead against my cheek. She apologized. I said nothing and kept rubbing her.

I felt into her and put a finger inside her vagina. She breathed hard behind her teeth just before she let out a quick, high-pitched squeal. She slipped a little and I grabbed her. Her body was shuddering and jolting.

"Oh... oh... oh... you have... you've got to stop," she said. "I don't know what just happened. What did you do to me?!"

She tried to catch her breath. "You... that..." she stuttered. "Was that supposed to happen?"

"You had an orgasm," I said.

"Oh my! I want another one---but not right now. I don't think I could handle another one right away. Oh my God. That was... where did you learn that?"

"*Those* movies," I said. "I didn't think that really happened, to be honest."

"Um... yeah... it's real!" Celia assured me. "How many girls have you done that to?"

"Just you."

"Liar."

"No. Just you. I've never made another girl come before. Like I said---I didn't think it was real."

Celia seemed quite proud that she'd been the one to shatter the myth, and also be the first girl I'd brought to orgasm. It was interesting how much control I had over her in that moment. It was a strange experience for both of us: physically for her and emotionally for me. We held each other tight as the water continued to cascade over us.

"Make love to me now," Celia begged.

"We don't have enough time," I said. "We've got to get out of here and get you back to Sarah's."

"No. We have time. Just be quick. You can do it fast, right?"

I brought myself up and slid inside her. We were making love again. I thrusted harder into her this time; she was still so tight, and it was still painful. It was difficult doing it standing up and the slippery surface of the tub made it even more of a challenge. It felt absolutely wonderful without a condom. We went for several minutes. I was nearing orgasm and debating whether I should come in her or not; the story about hot water killing sperm was untested. I pulled out and jerked myself off to come. It was quick. Celia and I watched my semen spiral between our feet and down the drain, followed by the swirling, pink clouds of her blood.

We finished in the shower and got out. We toweled off and got dressed. It was almost eight AM and we rushed to get our things around and return our room key.

The innkeeper was in the office and had a small plate with two Danishes on it sitting atop the desk.

"Are you kids hungry?" She asked. "These are some fine pastries. Oh! Look---there's two left! How perfect is that?"

"That is something," I said, as I placed the room key on the desk.

"Did you enjoy your stay?" The innkeeper asked.

"We did!" Celia said joyously.

"It was one of the best nights I can remember," I added.

"Well, that is wonderful! You two are such a cute pair," the innkeeper said. "You're going to be so happy in life together, I just know it! Kids like you give us old folks something to smile about: hope, love, oh---so many great things. I know love when I see it and you two... you just have it!" She gave us a bright, beautiful smile.

Celia blushed and giggled. She pulled her arms in tight. It was that gesture you make when you feel warm and gushy inside.

We bid the innkeeper goodbye and thanked her for the hospitality. She waved and told us to come back soon, and we said we'd try. Celia had an odd expression as she got into the car. She then motioned with her head: first toward her crotch and then toward the innkeeper. It took me a second to figure out what she was doing. I nodded and handed the innkeeper an additional twenty-dollar bill. She looked at it, and then looked at me, puzzled.

"It's for cleaning," I said. "We accidentally spilled some wine on the bed."

CHAPTER 14

I dropped Celia off at Sarah's and we kissed goodbye. I told her I'd call her later today and we could see about going out tonight. She said that would be fine and made her way into the house. I still found it strange that she used the front door without a problem, but that was between her and Sarah.

I drove home. I was hoping I didn't have to work today. I was very tired. Sleep had suddenly become high on my agenda. I pulled up to my house and sat in the car for a few minutes before going inside.

My mom was sitting at the table. She was reading the paper and having a cup of coffee.

"How was your night?" She asked. "Did you have a good time?"

I nodded and smiled. "It was great," I said. "Long, but pretty fun."

"Oh, what did you do?" She asked.

I lied my ass off. "I went to a few parties and caught up with some friends," I said. "I drank a little, so I slept at David's."

My mom shook her head. "You shouldn't drink, you know?" She said. "I'm glad you stayed at David's, though."

"How were the parties?" She asked.

"They were OK," I said. "Nothing to really pop a cork over."

My mom got a confused look on her face but said nothing.

I called into work and had the day off. I dragged myself to my room and fell on my bed like a stone. I slept the sleep of a dead man. I didn't wake up until five PM when my mom knocked on my door to tell me I had a phone call.

I went to take the call. "Hello?" I said.

"Hi," the voice on the other end said. It was Celia and she sounded downtrodden.

"What's wrong?" I asked. "You don't sound too great."

"I'm OK. I just miss you."

"I miss you, too. Can I see you tonight?"

"I'm not sure. I don't feel well. It's probably not a good idea."

"What's the matter?"

"I don't know. I may just be tired. I just got home from Sarah's a bit ago."

The conversation was getting cold and cryptic.

"Celia, are you in trouble?" I asked.

"No. I'm just..." she paused. "Can we talk tomorrow? I'm going to go to bed, I think."

"Sure. I'll call you in the afternoon. Maybe I'll take you to lunch if you're up to it."

Celia's voice sounded happier. "That would be nice," she said. "Talk tomorrow. I love you."

"I love you, too," I responded.

The phone clicked. There was no playful 'no, you hang up first' banter. Something was wrong and I had no idea what it could possibly be. I sat down in the chair by the phone and tried piecing things together. I replayed our entire night in my mind and other than a couple of awkward moments, it was fantastic.

I couldn't help but wonder if Celia had gotten in trouble with her folks, or if Sarah's parents had busted her for coming in so brazenly after eight AM and through the front door, at that. If that was the case, they'd had to have seen my car and known that Celia was with me, and...

I went to the kitchen and got a drink. My mom asked if I was alright. How was I supposed to answer her? *Yeah, I'm great. Hey, guess what, Celia and I are engaged. I lied to you and she lied to Sarah's folks and God knows who else. Oh, by the way, Celia and I had sex at a motel out of town...*

I looked at my mom and told her all was well.

I saw two letters with my name on them lying on the counter. They looked official. I didn't pick them up even though they were addressed to me.

"Mom, what are these letters?" I asked.

"Those came for you this afternoon. One is from school, the other is from the Air Force," she said in the most, motherly tone. "You should open them."

"I probably should. I don't know what school could be sending, I'm already set there," I said. "As for the Air Force---I'm definitely not talking to them."

I opened the letter from school and read it. It was a welcome note from my soon-to-be resident advisor. There were a couple of flyers and a poorly made sticker with the name and logo of the dorm where I'd be living. The flyers had pictures of students frolicking and enjoying *something*. Not one of them looked real: everyone was smiling too wide or had their mouth opened way too much in feigned excitement. The longer I studied the pictures, the less certain I felt about my decision to attend this school. Perhaps I should read what the *Boys in Blue* have to say?

I called Celia the next day and she was 'out with friends,' according to her brother. *Thanks, man.* I called back later, and her sister Patty and I talked for an hour. I liked Patty. I remember she had a crush on me for about a week during Freshman year. She was too mean to date: independent and very self-contained. Her boyfriend was a class-A stoner who had the intelligence of a brick and the common sense of a moth. I still can't believe Celia blazed with him.

Patty waited till the end of our conversation to tell me Celia was 'doing stuff' with their mom. *OK, I'll try again.*

Each time I called Celia was busy, not home or 'indisposed.' It was annoying and it went on for several days.

CHAPTER 15

A week had passed since Celia and I spent the night together and I hadn't seen her in all that time. I was missing her terribly and we'd only talked briefly once or twice. I think I'd talked to Patty longer than Celia over the week.

What was going on? There were so many things we had to do before I left, and Celia was holding it all up. I sounded selfish. It wasn't about what we had to do; it was about what we had *together*---did it still exist?

I sat in my room and looked at Celia's pictures. In one she was posed on her side on the floor, head in hand and propped with her elbow. That was my favorite. That was the picture I looked at the longest. It was the one most unlike Celia; this recent behavior was most unlike Celia. I stared at the picture without blinking and tears began to well in my eyes. A teardrop splattered on the photograph and I let it run down and taint the color.

"See what you made me do? You made me tarnish your beauty, my love," I said as the saline stream stopped about three quarters of the way down the photo.

I put the picture down and wiped my eyes. I was desperate and at my wit's end. I'd gone a week without seeing my true love and that was too long.

I pulled myself together and drove over to Celia's house. I was tired of looking at photographs, I had to see *her.* I had to know what was going on between us. I had to know if she still loved me.

I drove very fast. Celia hated me driving fast, it scared

her. She always knew if I'd driven fast even if she wasn't with me. She was probably at home right now working on her lecture for me: *'you drove ----- miles per hour to get here, didn't you?! You know how much I hate that. You're going to kill someone driving like that...'* I was perfectly OK with such a scolding---at least I'd get to hear her voice.

When I got to Celia's house, her brothers were out sitting on the curbside. Kenny---the elder of the two---gave me a nod and then pushed his younger brother aside.

"What it is, *Cheez Whiz?*" Kenny asked. The kid always had some weird rhyme to say.

"Ain't no thing, onion ring. Where's your sister?" I asked, in a slightly demanding tone.

"She's at the store with my mom, but they'll be back soon," he said. "Pull up a curb and tell me the good word."

I laughed. "Dude, where do you come up with this stuff?" I asked. "You're like Nipsey Russell or something, rhyming all the time."

"Dunno'. It's just something I do," Kenny responded. "The chicks like it."

"That's coz it's obnoxious and they feel sorry for you. You're a freakin' spaz."

"I'm a spaz with clazz that'll kick some azz---that's what I am."

"Or what you *wazz...*" Ricky, his younger brother chimed in.

I got up. "Good one, 'Rocko,'" I said. "I can't hang. You guys are too much for me. Is your dad around? I need a moment of his time."

"He's inside watching the game," Ricky said. "But he's probably toe-up. He's been drinking since noon."

"I'll make sure he's still alive," I said, as I walked into the house.

I heard strange snorts echoing off the high, cathedral ceiling in the living room. Sure enough, there was Celia's dad 'toe-up,' just as Ricky had said. I sat down on the couch adjacent to the chair he was sleeping in and made myself comfortable. I felt weird.

I'd been to Celia's house before and sat on this couch and been in this environment, but now it felt different. It felt unfamiliar. It felt as if I shouldn't be so comfortable---or be here at all.

As disturbing as it sounds, I watched Celia's dad toss and snort in his chair. It was hard not to. Big Kenny looked small, helpless and weak as he slept through the throes of an early afternoon bender. I could've killed him as he slept. I could've bestowed upon him what the Vietnam War failed to provide. I laughed at this ludicrous idea.

I thought about taking advantage of his state and asking for Celia's hand. He could answer in a drunken mumble and when the situation arose and he said I never asked, I would say I did---*and you said it was OK.* It was probably the safest way to do this, and the most cowardly. Common sense got the better of me and I chose to wait until he was awake and at least mildly sober.

I watched a little of the game. The volume was down. I wondered what the announcers were saying and what the score was. The Chicago White Sox were winning, though, because they looked happier than the Cleveland Indians.

I heard the door open, the sound of bags rustling and voices chattering in the kitchen. I heard Celia and a smile drew across my face. I stood up and waited, knowing that she'd come into the living room very soon. When she did, I was so happy to see her. However, the feeling didn't seem to be mutual.

"What are you doing here?" She asked. Her tone sounded as if I was forbidden from this place.

"I came to see you," I said. "You're never home when I call. I miss you."

"I've been busy, that's all."

"So, I've heard. It's been a week since we saw each other. It's too long to go without you. Can I take you to lunch or something so we can talk?"

"I already ate. We went for sandwiches after shopping."

Celia's dad snorted and groaned. It made the situation even more bizarre.

"OK, then can we go talk somewhere else?" I asked. "Somewhere not in front of your dad---who is totally blotto." I made a drinking motion.

"Sure," Celia said. "Let's go to my room. I've got to put a few things away,"

I hadn't been in Celia's bedroom in a while. She shared the room with her sister and I always found that strange; her brothers shared a room as well. It seemed such a Midwestern thing. We went in the room and closed the door. I sat on Celia's bed and watched her put her new clothes away.

"Those are nice," I commented.

Celia seemed to loosen up. She smiled and modeled her new outfits for me by holding them up to her body and moving from side to side. She looked so good---even better than before. Absence does indeed make the heart grow fonder. I had been missing her so much.

"What's been going on? Where have you been?" I asked. "It just seems so strange that we haven't done anything since..."

"I know. It's not anything..." Celia paused. "It's just me."

"I don't understand."

"I'm all out of sorts. After we had sex, I was just like..."

"Like what?"

"I don't know. I loved it, it was so amazing... you were so good to me and made me feel like a princess---or even better. I just... I just didn't feel *the same* afterward, you know?"

"You *weren't* the same. You lost your virginity. Baby, that's huge! I can't even imagine what that must be like to go from here to there. I guess that's something guys just take for granted. We lose ours, but it's... yeah... not even close. It's just semantics."

"That's it! I can't figure out why I'm so messed up. It's a big deal, but it happens every day. It's part of life. It was going to happen to me at some point, but why do I feel like I did something wrong?"

Celia began to cry. I came to her and took her in my arms. She shook as she cried. I'd never heard her sob like this and the tighter I held her, the harder she cried.

"Oh my God, I'm so sorry," she said through her tears. "What's wrong with me?"

I stroked her hair and tried to shush her. "There's nothing wrong with you my love," I said. "I think you just give yourself too big of a moral compass and too stern of values. That's all."

"That makes me sound like a nun, or something. I'm not like that, am I? I'm not a total prude, am I?!" She asked, still crying but calming down.

"No. Now you're just like every other girl whose lost her virginity and is confused about it," I said. "You certainly can't be a nun or a prude anymore."

Celia pulled back and wiped her tear-swollen face. She laughed at my observation and gently tapped her shaking fists into my shoulders.

"Great. Now I'm a slut. I hate you!" She said, as she rubbed her nose on my shirt. "There. You've got my germs now. That's what you get for calling me a hussy."

I didn't say anything, I just kissed her. I hadn't felt her lips on mine for a week and it felt like the first time we'd kissed. Our tongues lightly and timidly touched as if we'd never French kissed before. I could feel Celia's body go limp. I held her close and just listened to the sounds of our breathing and kissing. When we stopped, my head was light and buzzy. I felt slightly drunk.

"Wow. Where'd that come from?" She asked, swooning.

"From us," I said, swooning as well. "Promise me: no more *breaks?* I don't think I can handle it."

"Me either. I feel like I did from that wine."

"Me too. Maybe even more so."

Celia put her head to my chest. "You said I was a hussy." She noted.

I laughed. "No, *you* said you were a hussy---and a slut," I replied.

"I'm your slut… and your hussy. Don't you forget it."

"Never."

"That's what I want to hear," Celia said, smiling seductively.

She stepped back and began unbuttoning her blouse. I looked around the room. The curtains were open, and the door was unlocked---we were *not* doing this here, were we?

"Take your clothes off," Celia whispered. "I want to make love."

"Here?!" I asked, in a panicked whisper.

"Uh huh. On the floor. Come on."

I was absolutely stunned. We hadn't seen each other in a week. In the first five minutes of meaningful communication we'd had over that time, all signs pointed to a possible break-up. And now *this?* What was happening? It was like some odd sort of make-up or redemption sex---or whatever. Regardless of what it was, it couldn't happen here. *Not here. Not now.*

I was fully dressed, but Celia had stripped down to her underwear. I kept looking at the window. Anyone in the backyard or walking the perimeter of the fence could see us. I didn't take a second look at the door. I knew it was unlocked. I knew Patty---or anybody---could walk into this room without warning and we would be in trouble.

"Why are you still dressed?" Celia asked. Her voice sounded suggestive.

"Why are you *not?!*" I wondered aloud.

My thoughts and vision were bouncing between the window, the possibility of an unwanted walk-in and Celia in her red, lacy lingerie---an ensemble I'd never seen before. I was being driven crazy in every different direction.

"What are you afraid of?" Celia asked teasingly. The more she talked, the more she sounded like a temptress.

I shook my head in disbelief. "What am *I* afraid of? Where do I start?" I asked. "Let's see: your dad, your mom---your siblings; the possibility that any one---or *all* of them---could come through that door; the fact that the curtains are open---I'm sure there's more, but that's just the *knowns* at the moment." I could feel my forehead begin to bead with sweat.

"Now, who has the big moral compass and stern values?" Celia asked mockingly.

"It's not about that. It's..." I said, trailing off.

Celia undid my belt, put her hand into my pants and began stroking me. My underwear was sticky. This wasn't helping the situation.

"Ooh, you're wet..." Celia said, as she licked her lips.

She leaned close and whispered in my ear, "You want to fuck me now. Come on. Fuck me. You won't make love, so let's be adventurous and fuck. Fuck me on my sister's bed."

It was still jaw-dropping to hear Celia say the word 'fuck.' It grated on me, but it sounded so hot as well. When she said it, she wasn't herself. At this moment, she was definitely not herself at all.

"Honey, no. Not now. Please stop..." I said. I grabbed Celia's arm to get her to stop stroking me. I ejaculated into my underwear and all over her hand. It felt so good, but *I* felt so awful. I finally understood how Celia was feeling earlier about losing her virginity: it was going to happen, it was right, but perhaps just not the right *time.*

Celia's head was down. She rolled her eyes up and looked at me. She looked so devilish. I'd never seen her this way before. The fact she was wearing lacy, red underwear, had just jerked me off and said 'fuck' a bunch of times only served to amp the devilishness.

We were silent. It was an uncomfortable silence at that. I looked down at my pants. My briefs were thick with semen and I could smell it. I was hoping it would not penetrate the fabric and be visible through my jeans. I looked at Celia and her expression had changed. She looked like herself again. She peered around. She seemed to be in total shock that she was in her underwear and had her hand in mine.

"I'm sorry," she said. "I don't know what happened."

"I think I do," I replied. "It was all that *slut talk.*"

"Don't make jokes. You came in my hand."

"In my underwear, too. Your hand will wash. Besides, you did it to me."

"I know... I'm... what are we going to do?"

"We just need a dirty t-shirt or something---something to wipe everything up with."

Celia withdrew her hand from my pants very slowly. She was careful not to make the mess any bigger. Once her hand was free, she dug through her laundry hamper for a t-shirt. I stepped over to the door and quietly turned the lock.

Celia rubbed the semen from her hand. She put her clothes back on and waited for me to clean up. I pulled my jeans down a bit and stuffed the shirt into my underwear. I blindly swept and pulled until I felt I'd gotten it all. Nothing soaked through, but the smell was still prevalent, and my underwear was wet. I grabbed a bottle of Celia's perfume and shot a quick spritz of it into my underwear.

"This is going to cause a few looks," I said.

"You smell like me," Celia stated.

"It's better than the alternative. No matter what, some-one's going to notice something."

"You shouldn't stop and talk to anyone when you leave."

"At least not anyone at crotch level," I responded sarcas-tically.

Celia and I walked stealthily out of her room. We moved easily through the house and avoided everyone. When we got outside, we breathed a collective sigh of relief.

"Can we get together tonight?" I asked. "Maybe get some dinner or something?"

"I think so," she said. "You know I've missed you, too. It's just been weird, you know... everything."

"I do know. You seem to have developed a craving, but don't want to give in entirely just yet," I explained. "It'll just get better from here, my love."

"I believe that. I really do! I want you to make love to me

again---and soon!" Celia said, her body language shifting from pure to sinful. "I should probably apologize again for my behavior. That... that thing I just did to you. I don't know where all that stuff came from. It's like I was switching between bodies, you know? Maybe when we made love you broke something in me?"

I looked dead at her. "Just your Hymen," I said.

"Gross!" Celia said. She punched me hard in the chest and knocked me back a bit.

I was starting to get into my car when Tina, Celia's mom, came outside and gave me a bit of harassment.

"Where you going, *slickness?* You too good to talk to us country folk?" Tina asked, lighting a cigarette.

"He has to go, momma," Celia said. "He'll be back tonight. We're going to dinner."

"Why don't you cook something for him, *Snowdrop?* She can cook pretty well, you know?"

"I'll cook something for him, soon. He knows I can make food. I used to bring him sandwiches and desserts in school when he worked on his articles for the paper."

"She did, and they were great!" I asserted.

"Oh, you have to say that, coz momma's here," Tina chided.

"Momma!" Celia said, embarrassed.

"Nope, it's true girly. A man will say the damndest things to win a female over," Tina stated. "This one here's a real charmer, too."

Celia blushed. "Momma, stop," she said.

"It's OK. I enjoy the flattery. It *is* flattery, isn't it?" I asked, slightly uncertain.

"Sure, it is. I like you, *Rollo,*" Tina said. "You make my Snowdrop happy and that's all that matters to a mother: that her babies are happy."

With that I was ready to leave. I could only take Celia's family all together in very small doses.

Her mom was a complete head case and a mystery. She ran hot and cold with me and I couldn't tell if she liked me or not.

She called Celia 'Snowdrop' because she was so pale. I remember her saying once that when Celia was born, it looked like a giant, bloody snowball dropped out of her. She had names for the other kids, too. She called Celia's sister Patty 'Petunia,' and the boys were 'K.J.' (Kenny Junior) and 'Rocky' (Ricky). I had no idea what she called Big Kenny, other than 'that lump I sleep with.' She called me 'Slickness' and 'Rollo'---after the candy, I think. Somehow, I was lucky enough to get two nicknames.

Celia gave me a quick kiss goodbye. Her mother was still outside, thus making a real kiss a little awkward.

"I love you," she said.

"I love you, too," I responded.

"Sorry about momma, you know... she's just..."

"*Momma...*" I said with a bad southern accent.

Celia laughed and said, "That's terrible---accurate, but terrible!"

"I'll call you later," I said. "Think of where you want to go and eat, OK?"

"Sure. Love you."

"Love you, too," I said, as I backed out of the driveway and headed home.

Celia and I went out for dinner. The vibe was strange during the entire meal. I took her dancing afterward and even though we danced a lot, Celia seemed out of it. She was quiet and when she did talk, it was as if she didn't listen to what I'd said; just drawing random answers from a box. It was frustrating. I didn't understand any of what was going on, nor did I realize it was the sign of things to come.

CHAPTER 16

I'd seen Celia only a few times since our dinner date. Each time was either tense and uncomfortable, or quiet and reserved. There were a couple of fights thrown in as well---just to balance it all out. We'd gone a week or so at a time with maybe a phone call or two, or a quick date. It was as if our relationship was falling apart and I had no idea why.

When I tried to touch Celia, she'd be lukewarm. It felt as if she was 'allowing' me access to her. She was shutting me out of everything and it was killing me.

I called her up one evening and asked if I could come and see her. I told her I wanted to go to the park and sit on the swings like we used to. I wanted to sit on the swings and talk like we used to. I wanted to hold hands on the swings like we used to. I wanted us to be us---just like we used to. We hadn't been to the park to swing for a while and I missed it. Moreover, I just missed *her*.

On the drive to her house, I wondered which Celia I was going to be with tonight: would it be the unsophisticated, angelic, soft-touch romantic Celia, or the overtly amorous, hot-button, hellcat Celia? I was currently dealing with a distant, cold and invisible version of her. I realize that sex changes a person, but I didn't realize those changes could be so dramatic and drastic. I placed a great deal of the blame on myself.

For as much as I was fascinated with the new, adventurous model, there were so many things about the old Celia---*my Celia*---that I missed greatly. This was the Celia I fell in love with.

My Celia talked about all the things she'd missed out on

and longed for as a kid but knew she could have them again and pass them on to her own child.

My Celia would rather spin giddily in the torrent of a rainstorm than seek shelter from it. She said she hated seeing 'God's tears' go to waste.

My Celia wore pretty dresses and cute outfits that she'd made---not lacy, red, store bought lingerie---*although, I'm not complaining about that.*

My Celia found the stupidest things intriguing and could give a valid reason why; before you realized it---you'd be agreeing with her.

My Celia loved country music. Sometimes if I stepped out and left her in the car, she'd secretly tune the country station in on my radio. Later, on my drive home, I'd get treated to some *caterwaulin' twang.* For as bad as it was, I'd always smile and think of her.

My Celia loved to be kissed on her cheeks. She loved the feel of my lips and tip of my tongue touching her cheeks more than on her lips.

My Celia made the best strawberry shortcakes. She made the cakes and the compote from scratch. Her cakes were always rich and buttery; the compote sweet and loaded with berries.

My Celia loved macaroni and cheese even though she hadn't had it in years. Her mother refused to buy it or make it, saying it reminded her of their 'poor days.' She wouldn't eat it anymore, either, but she still loved it. My Celia...

My Celia loved *me.* At least, I was hoping she still did.

When I arrived at her house, she was waiting outside on the curb. She had a small basket beside her. I parked and got out. She walked over to me and put her hand out.

"Hi," she said. "I made you something."

I smiled. "I can smell them," I said.

I opened the basket. Inside were two perfect, rich buttery-smelling shortcakes and two small containers of strawberry compote.

"You know me too well," I said. I took a deep breath and

smelled the wonderful aroma of the shortcakes.

"I thought you'd forgotten about them," she said.

"No. There's no way. I have dreams about these."

"When you're not dreaming about me?"

"I have dreams of you making them!"

"Anything for my guy. What am I wearing?"

"An apron."

"And..."

"One of those poofy chef's hats."

"Well, at least I've got a hat on," Celia said, as she leaned in and kissed my cheek.

I closed my eyes tight for a second. I held back the welling tears.

I looked at Celia. "I've missed you so much. You have no idea what it's been like," I said. "I've been busy and putting in extra time at work to keep my mind off of whatever is happening to us."

"Let's go to the park," Celia said. "We can talk on the way."

We held hands like we did when we started dating; arms gently swinging, carefree and lively; innocent and without pretense---like the young lovers we are, but for some reason, were trying to age.

We were quiet to start. The crickets chirping and the warm July breeze waltzing with the leaves was an ambiance not to be disturbed. The night sky was filled with stars. They twinkled above our head and dropped onto the horizon. We were surrounded by them and the black background of the night.

"I've been thinking," Celia said suddenly. "You're going to leave me soon."

"No. I'm not *leaving* you," I assured her. "I'm just going to school. I'll be able to visit."

"No. You're truly leaving me. You're going to school, but it's somewhere else. Somewhere that's *not here*. Somewhere far away and I won't be there."

"Don't say it like that. When you say it like that, it sounds like we'll never see each other again."

"I don't want that."

"Neither do I. I wish I didn't have to go to school at all."

Celia stopped and looked at me. "Why don't you tell your folks you don't want to go?" She said. "Stay here. You told me you weren't ready yet, tell them too."

"I already have. I'd told them that from the start," I said. "They weren't having it. I had to decide between school and the military. I chose the one I felt was better suited for me, though neither of them really is." I sounded like an angry little boy

"What are we going to do?" Celia asked.

"First, we're going to go swing. After that, we're going to talk about us," I said. "Most importantly, we're going to stop this no communication; out of sight/ out of mind thing. We're engaged, damn it. We're lovers. We're not supposed to be apart."

"But we *will* be apart. You can't say we won't and have it be true. You're leaving."

"We will be 'apart,' my love, but not like we have been. This no calls, no dates, no seeing each other isn't us. I'll be away, but I'll always be here," I said as I pointed to Celia's heart. "I won't let the distance tear us apart. You have to do the same. Promise me you will."

Celia nodded. "I promise, my love. I promise. I do," she said as her eyes began to tear.

We continued walking. When we reached the park, I set the basket down on the grass next to the swings. I helped Celia on and gave her a soft push. She pulled and pushed the chains to go higher; her legs straight out; her hair blowing forward and back.

I watched her swing and ate one of the shortcakes. Celia loved the swings. She loved the swings more than anything: more than pizza; more than milkshakes; more than her new-found affinity for sex---maybe even more than me. She always said that the swings made her feel 'free,' and 'young.'

I didn't talk to Celia for several minutes when she started to swing. She always asked why I didn't join her until later, but

I never told her. I didn't want to interrupt her time to be with the little girl she never was. The swings made her feel like she wanted. The swings helped her fill that hole created by her lack of a proper childhood.

As she glided through the air, she looked so happy, so innocent and so young. I couldn't begin to fathom what she was actually thinking and feeling on that swing, because I couldn't fathom what it was like for her growing up. She'd told me things. I listened, but never fully comprehended them. How could I? I grew up in a safe home with two siblings and two loving parents. My dad had a steady job. We'd only moved twice in my eighteen years of life. My mom was a teacher and she made sure we stayed straight and well-versed. My folks provided well for me, my older brother and my little sister. They made sure we didn't go without, and always appreciated what we had.

Conversely, Celia's life was hard. She didn't say a lot about it, but it was painfully obvious. I didn't understand the way her parents acted toward each other. I didn't know why they seemed to love her brothers more than her and her sister. It explained why her sister was mean. It explained why Celia was subservient and eager to please.

Celia's mom made things. She sewed and crocheted and passed those skills onto Celia. She also enjoyed arts and crafts and painted as a hobby. She scoffed my artwork and always told me my talents would 'come in handy one sunny day.' She was a sarcastic cunt.

Her dad was a boozer who bounced from construction job to construction job. The family's moves paralleled her dad getting fired. He liked sports, especially baseball. He loved the Cleveland Indians. No one could bad mouth 'The Tribe.' He was a good pitcher and had played well in high school but got drafted and the Vietnam War swallowed him up. When it spat him back out, he was never the same again.

I think Celia's dad liked me. He always patted my shoulder and laughed when I won a hand of cards. He said my name sounded 'important.' Sometimes I'd see him in the garage before

I'd go home, and he'd be drunk. He'd call me over and tell me to be good to Celia---to be good *for* her. He told me to take her away from 'this,' and make sure she had everything she needed. He was a man who could never truly be proud. He was a man who was always defeated.

Celia's voice snapped me from my daze. "Come swing with me now," she said playfully.

I got up and sat in the swing next to her. We held hands and swung together for a few minutes.

"Did you enjoy the shortcake?" Celia asked.

"Yes, I did. It was probably the best you've ever made," I said.

"I love making things for you, you know?"

"I know. You always treat me so well. I just can't help but feel bad about things."

"Like what? What's there to feel bad about?"

I slowed our swinging down so we could talk. I didn't want to mix present troubles with something that helped Celia reconcile her past. I felt I'd possibly damaged her enough already.

"I'm sorry Celia---about everything that has been going on lately," I said, looking at the ground.

Celia tugged at my hand and pulled me toward her, trying to get me to look at her.

"You don't have to apologize for anything," she said. "I've been acting so weird since we made love. I never thought it'd be so complicated... the feelings and all. Becoming a woman wasn't a simple transition, I guess."

"I don't know. You're the first girl I've slept with who's gone to extremes," I said. "But you're also the first girl I've slept with who I truly loved. Maybe it happened with the others, too but I just didn't pay attention."

"I think I'm just afraid, you know?" Celia said.

"Afraid of what?"

"Everything: making love and how it made me feel; changes in my life; your going away to school; what might happen to us---stuff I can't even imagine. I don't know. I just know it's making me crazy."

The concerns we had were valid but seemed to be getting blown out of proportion. We just needed to sit down and figure things out. We needed to remember that our love for each other was stronger than anything we would face.

"We just need to untie the little knots in our life, that's all," I said. "There's a lot going on, but we can handle it."

"I want to marry you right now," Celia said out of the blue. "That's one knot I *would* like to see tied!"

I laughed. "Very soon, my love," I said. "I still haven't asked your dad for your hand yet. I have to do that. Big Kenny would have my balls if I didn't have his permission."

"You could ask him tonight."

"Do you think he's ready to hear it?"

"I don't think any father is, but my daddy likes you, he really does. You'll be fine."

I had to think. I know I had to carry out this tradition, but I wasn't sure if I was really ready to do it at the moment. I just knew it had to be done and I knew it had to be done before I left for school.

"Let's swing some more, Celia."

We walked back to Celia's house and talked about random things, none of them dealt with sex, marriage or how weird things have been lately. As we walked, I could feel Celia's hand becoming slightly damp with perspiration. It was as if the old Celia had returned. However, the new Celia was present as well. The old Celia would've pulled her hand away in embarrassment---tonight she didn't let it bother her.

Celia's house was dark and quiet when we got there. We didn't realize how late it was. Everyone had gone to bed. I breathed a quick sigh of relief---I'd bought another day to muster the courage to talk to her dad.

"Drat!" Celia said. "You'll have to wait till tomorrow to get daddy's permission."

"Damn the luck!" I said, shaking my fist in mock anger.

I held up the basket. "Can I take home the other short-cake?" I asked.

"Yes, silly," Celia said. "I made them for you."

"I didn't want to be selfish, that's all."

"I made extra for my family. Those were yours," she said with a smile.

I set the basket on the hood of my car and went to kiss Celia goodnight. I pulled her to me and kissed her softly on the cheek. I heard her giggle as my tongue touched her delicate flesh. I kissed her other cheek the same way and she giggled again.

"You haven't done that in a while," Celia said.

"I know how much you like it," I responded.

"Did I ever tell you that?"

"No, I just always knew from your reaction when I did it."

"It's very nice. For some reason, it always makes me feel loved. I can't explain it. It's so silly. I just need to stop talking..."

I moved in and kissed Celia's lips. She pushed her mouth tightly to mine in a way she never had before. Our kissing went from subtle and slow to aggressive and animalistic.

Celia ran her fingernails hard down the back of my shirt. She'd never done this. I pulled away and Celia caught my bottom lip between her teeth. She slowly shook her head as if to tell me 'no' and continued biting softly on my lip.

Celia opened her mouth and let go. She had that devilish look on her face again and I wasn't sure what was going to happen next.

"I don't know where that came from," I said half joking.

"I do. It's all, your fault, you know," she said with a sinister smile.

"Are you saying I've corrupted you?"

"Oh yes, and I want you to corrupt me even more."

"Anything you wish," I said. I moved toward her and we kissed again.

Celia pulled away and started kissing my neck. It was driving me crazy. I was getting hard very quickly.

"My God, you have to stop," I said. "I'm so hard right now... I want you so bad."

Celia spoke while she kissed me. "Take it out," she said. "I'll give you head."

I was dumbfounded. "What? Here?" I asked in a panic.

"Yeah. Right here."

"We're outside!"

"OK, in the car then. Let's get in your car. Let's go---right now."

We stumbled to my car. I helped Celia into the backseat and climbed on top of her. We continued to savagely kiss. I undid my pants and pulled myself out. I sat back and Celia took her blouse and pants off. She was in just her bra and panties.

She dropped down onto the floor of the car and took me into her mouth. Celia sucked hard and slow. With every motion I felt like I was going to explode. The first time she went down on me was amazing---*this was astronomical.*

I took my shirt off while she gave me head and I draped it over the driver's seat.

I watched Celia's head bobbing in my crotch. Her hair brushing on my skin and the feeling of being in her mouth was becoming too much to take. I was ready to come.

"Celia I'm going to come," I said.

She pulled her head up. "I don't care," she mumbled and dropped back on me.

"You don't want me to shoot off in your mouth," I said.

She kept going and I was so close to climax.

"Celia, please. You have to stop," I begged. "You don't want to taste that stuff."

She didn't stop and when I tried to push her off me, she sucked harder and faster and wrapped her arms tightly around my waist. I couldn't move. She had me locked up and each time I tried to get away, she pushed, wrapped, or squeezed making it impossible for me to escape.

I took a quick, deep breath, gritted my teeth and pushed my hips up as I ejaculated into Celia's mouth. She continued sucking even after I'd come. I could feel my semen trickling from her mouth and onto my leg. I grabbed my shirt and held it for her.

She stopped and didn't say a word. She took the shirt from me, covered her mouth and wiped her face. She cleaned off my penis and legs as well. I didn't know what to think.

"You didn't swallow that did you?" I asked.

She didn't say a word. She turned and looked at me and slowly slinked toward my face. She grabbed the back of my head and pulled me to her. She kissed me full on the mouth. She forced her tongue between my lips. I could taste the remnants of my semen in her mouth. It tasted so weird. I wasn't sure what to make of any of this. It was all too surreal.

"Celia. I'm so sorry," I said. "I told..." she pressed her finger to my lips and shushed me.

"You wanted to do that," she said. "*I* wanted you to do that. I told you I wanted to taste you."

"I know but..."

"Stop talking about it. You needed to let yourself lose control. I wanted to take you someplace you'd never been."

"You certainly did."

"What did it feel like to finish in my mouth?" Celia asked. "Was it like finishing in my vagina, or was it different?

"I'm not sure," I said. "When we made love the first time I had on a condom; the second time, I pulled out and finished myself."

"Maybe we need to solve some mysteries then," she said. "I'd like to know. *Enquiring minds want to know!*"

"How do you propose we do that? Solve these mysteries?" I asked, still unsure of everything.

Celia pulled herself up and slid to the passenger's side of the seat. She took off her bra and panties and sat naked on the black, hardened vinyl. She brought her knees up to her chest and spread her legs.

"There's only one way," she said. "Make love to me."

I looked around. "Here? Geez, we've already taken one risk tonight," I said. "Don't you think we should do this later? And perhaps somewhere else? We're parked in front of your house!"

"I don't care. Everyone's asleep," she said. "It's like two AM and... let's just do it. No one can see us."

I wanted to. I wanted to make love to her so badly, but once again, I was having trouble with Celia's new-found sense of adventure and sudden exhibitionism. Earlier, I'd reminisced about my pure, chaste, innocent Celia, and how I longed for her return. The Celia who I took to the park to swing tonight was who I wished was here right now. This she-devil, sex pot, slut-in-training sitting in the back of my car scared me to death and I didn't know how to handle her.

"Can we try another time?" I asked. "Why don't we go out tomorrow? Afterwards, we can go to my house. My family will be gone. We can at least do it in my bed."

"No. Here. Now. I want you. I want you to make love to me right now. I want to feel you inside me." Celia said in a seductive tone. I could feel my resistance waning.

"I don't have a condom," I said.

"You don't need one," she responded.

"I think I do. There's... well... you know?"

"Uh-uh. Come on, I'm right here. I'm so ready for you."

I felt my willpower fading. I knew this was neither the time nor the place, but I wanted to make love. I wanted to be inside her. I wanted to feel her around me. I wanted her to feel me filling her. I slid toward her. My erection was so rigid it was as if every ounce of blood in my body went straight to my sex. I felt light-headed, like I was going to pass out.

Celia giggled seductively as I came closer. "That's it, my love. I'm right here," she said.

I pressed myself against her and pushed into her body with no regard for anything but making love to her. She moaned out as I thrusted in her. She wrapped her legs around my waist and slid down on the seat. I could tell she was still hurting.

I let out a strange groan I swear I'd never made in my life. We'd had sex without protection once before. It felt amazing, but it was not like this. This time the pleasure I was experiencing was beyond comprehension.

I pulled her tight to me and breathed hard as I thrusted and grinded into her. She began to pant. She was having trouble catching her breath. Words like 'yes,' and 'God,' and 'love me,' were the only intelligible things she said.

We'd been making love for almost fifteen minutes. We were wearing out.

"Are you OK, baby?" I asked, huffing my words.

"Yes... I'm amazing," she responded in a whisper.

"You are *so amazing*," I said. "But are you ready to stop?"

"No. You're not finished yet. You have to finish. We have to know..."

"That doesn't matter. That's not even..."

"No. You can't stop. You can't..."

"I have to."

"No, you don't. You don't. I want you to keep going." Celia pressed her mouth to my ear and said, "I want you to get me pregnant."

All of a sudden everything that made sense was gone. The morals of the world; the traditions I was supposed to uphold; the respect I was taught to have for people, places and things ceased to exist. I thrust and pushed as deep as I could into Celia, ejaculating inside of her. Her eyes widened. It was as if she could feel my semen fill her vagina. My ass clenched tight as I pushed hard and forced every drop out of me and into her.

"My God!" Celia cried. "I don't know what to say."

We fell together and lay on the backseat of my car: naked, sweat-soaked and possibly fertilized. I kissed Celia gently on the lips. It was a delicate, lover's kiss and even though I was still deep inside of her, coated in semen and so far from purity and virtue---I felt like I was kissing the old Celia again.   "I love you, Celia Beth," I said in a whisper.

"I love you, too Roland Jacob," she responded.

"We used middle names. I think we're married."

Celia chuckled. "You're going to marry me now. You just have to!" She said, over-accentuating her mild southern drawl.

"I don't want this to end. You have to leave me. I like you being here. Why don't you stay?" Celia asked. She sounded as if she was in a state of pure bliss and pulling out of her would destroy this rapture.

I felt like I had to be the voice of reason. "You have to go in. I have to get home," I said. "If we don't get into some kind of trouble, we're the luckiest people alive."

"I know. It sucks," she stated. "We have to do this again---very soon."

"*Very* soon."

We cleaned up a little and got dressed. Obviously, I did not put my shirt back on. So many things were running through my mind and I had to imagine it was the same for Celia. We didn't say much as we tried to get out of the car as quietly as possible. I walked Celia to the front door and kissed her goodnight.

"There'll be more nights like this, I promise," I said.

"There'd better be," she replied.

I stared at Celia; her face half-lit from the glow of the streetlight. She was so beautiful. My head was still in a spin from what just happened. I could've said anything to her right now, something romantic, something tender---instead I blurted out: "I have to know---did you swallow it?"

Celia looked sideways and touched her chin. "I'm not going to say," she said. "You can mill that in your head---it'll have to be the stuff of your dreams."

"I don't know what to believe anymore," I remarked.

"OK, well, I'm going to go in and go to bed. Drive home safe. No speeding!"

"I promise I won't. I'd hate to get pulled over shirtless."

Celia laughed and touched my bare chest. She gave me a quick kiss and started toward the front door. Just before she walked into the house, I stopped her.

"I have to ask you one more thing," I said.

"What's that?" She asked.

"How did it feel for you?"

CHAPTER 17

It had been two weeks since Celia and I turned my car into a den of iniquity and once again---I was missing her terribly. We'd talked very briefly and seen each other even less in those fourteen days. I was starting to stress. I'd heard excuse after excuse, and some were so far-fetched I didn't even bother to argue or ask. I was devastated. Everyone knew it, but no one asked why. If they had, I didn't know what I'd say: make up some lie, or tell the truth?

My parents and I fought constantly. My dad didn't understand what I was going through, and my mom didn't want to hear about it.

My brother Jerry tried to counsel and console me. He told me he 'knew what I was dealing with,' and that 'girls are hard to figure out.' *Yes,* to the latter and *I don't think so* to the former. My big brother had always been more interested in school than girls. The one girl he'd dated seriously was really more of a 'study buddy.' I'm sure she wanted him to *open his books* a little more, but he'd rather focus on the commonwealth of West Virginia than the complexities of a wet vagina. I didn't need his advice, but I didn't tell him that.

My little sister Devon was lost completely. She liked Celia a lot and they did things together. It was weird. Celia's child-like qualities came out when she was around my sister; while conversely, Devon acted more mature. They talked about so many odd things, I couldn't keep up. Devon would always ask when Celia was coming back over, and Celia would always make sure she took time out to spend with her. That wasn't happening now.

I spent most of my days working. If I wasn't working, I was finalizing things for school. I was set to leave in less than a week and if I hadn't wanted to go before, I *really* didn't want to go now. I feared that I would get on that plane, jet off to college and never see Celia again. I didn't want to lose her, yet I could feel it happening. *Why was it happening? What did I do? What can I do to fix it? Where are you my love? I need you so bad.*

The phone rang and I ran to answer it. It had to be Celia. I picked up the handset and said hello. It was a wrong number. Just another disappointment.

I wanted to go to Celia's house and see her. I knew she had to be there. I had to see her. This was ridiculous. We were in love. We were engaged. We'd had sex. I hadn't asked her dad for her hand yet. We were still getting married, right? There were too many questions and they all needed answers.

I called Celia's house and got her sister Patty. Patty rambled on about something. I tuned out most of it. I just wanted to know if Celia was home. Patty said she wasn't, but I knew that was bullshit. I said I was coming over and the story changed. She said Celia was sick in bed. I wanted to say she was sick in bed because she was pregnant, but I didn't. I asked Patty if I could speak to her. She sighed and relented. There was a pause and then I heard Celia's groggy voice.

"What?" She asked coldly.

"Celia, it's me. It's Rollie," I said.

"I know. How are you?"

"I'm not good, but maybe I'm better than you."

"I'm sick. I've got the flu and it's bad," she said as she coughed.

"I want to see you," I said. "Can I see you?"

"Not right now. I'm so sick, baby. I've been like this for a few days."

"How long is 'a few days'?"

"A couple. It doesn't matter. I'm sick and it sucks."

"I can imagine. What can I do to make you feel better? I'll go and get you something. Tell me what you need, and I'll bring it to you. I want to see you. I just want to be with you. I just want to hold your hand. I don't care if you're sick. That's part of the vows: in sickness and in health."

Celia coughed again and it sounded awful. "Listen, I've got to go," she said. "I think I'm going to throw up."

"I'm so sorry, my love. Please let me come and see..."

The receiver clicked before I could finish my sentence. The low, cold buzz of the dial tone made me want to bash the handset into something---either the wall or my head.

I hung up the phone and burst into tears. What just happened? Why did she shut me out at a time when she needed someone---*when she needed her lover*---to comfort her and help nurse her back to health? Why was she doing this to me?

A little voice in my head mocked me. It said that she was faking being sick. She'd hung up the phone and she---and her family---were having a laugh at my expense. They laughed at my pleas to her; how pathetic and needy I sounded. They joked about me and my family and how much they despised us; how we thought we were better than them, and that we had 'better stuff.' They offered to get Celia an abortion. They talked about going against all their old-fashioned values and Catholic Doctrine to ensure that Celia got rid of the baby she was carrying---*my baby*. These are the things the little voice told me, and they kept getting louder and louder.

"FUCK!" I yelled. "No. This is not real!"

I got in my car and headed toward Celia's house, but did not get there. I turned into the court a block away from where she lived. I pulled into a random driveway and broke down. A couple of kids were playing in the yard. I saw them as I pulled up, but I didn't pay them much more attention.

One of them tapped on my window. I could hear his little squeaky voice through the glass.

"You OK, mister?" He asked.

I rolled the window down and shook my head.

"I ain't alright, kiddo," I said, as I wiped the tears from my eyes. "Don't ever fall in love, OK. Promise me that?"

"Love is yucky," he said emphatically.

The other kid interjected, "Yeah, love will give you *cooties.*"

The first kid added, "Yeah and diarrhea and stuff. You don't want that."

I laughed and wagged my finger. "No, my man, you definitely *do not* want that," I said.

I told the kids to "stay young and have fun." They started doing goofy kid things---basically spazzing out. It made me smile. I backed out of the driveway and drove off. I didn't go to Celia's. I went to get food. I found myself at one of the local pizza joints we frequented. I went in and ordered a pizza for one and a chocolate milkshake. It was Tuesday.

The night before I left for school, I called Celia. I'd been praying that I could see her one more time before I left. My faith tested and failed---one more reason not to believe in God. We talked on the phone, but it wasn't right. Nothing was right.

"I promise I'll write every day," Celia said. Her words sounded cynical and rehearsed.

"I want to see you before I leave. Please, my love," I begged.

"I'll come to the airport tomorrow, OK? We can say our goodbyes there."

"I told you it's not really 'goodbye.' It's just a short time away."

"You're still going away, still leaving me---it's goodbye to me."

"Do you miss me? I miss you every second of every day."

"I do. I miss you."

"I love you, Celia."

"I love you, too. We're going to get married."

I swallowed hard and said to myself, *I want to believe that.*

"Yes, we are---and I can't wait," I said. My words sounded hollow. "How are you feeling?"

"I'm better," she said. "Don't I sound better?"

"You totally do." I said, but I needed more information. "How's everything else?"

"Like what?" She wondered.

I sighed. I didn't want to ask anything directly. I tap-danced around the subject.

"Just *everything*," I said.

"Everything is fine," she said. "I'm tired, love. I'll see you tomorrow."

"OK. Goodnight Celia Beth, I love you so much. I can't wait to see you."

"Goodnight."

She hung up. No 'I love you.' No use of my middle---or first name for that matter. No nothing. I just got an empty promise and a tepid fuzzy---she couldn't even warm it up for me. I didn't know what to do. I was so lost. All I could think of was those kids from a couple days ago and their take on love: 'cooties, and diarrhea and stuff.' *Absolutely freakin' right.*

I woke up the next morning and looked around my room. With the exception of a couple of random pictures from magazines I'd stuck on the wall, my bed and my desk---the place was cleared out. Everything essential that I owned had been shipped to my uncle's house to be stored and ready for me when I moved up to school and into my dorm room.

My room---this place I'd spent the last six years of my life. This place I'd hated for months after we'd moved here because it was new and not *my room* and never would be.

This place where I studied the craft of authors and aesthetic of painters; where I'd listen to music by day and fantasized of stardom by night, only to realize I was just a hopeless romantic with inconceivable dreams. This place where I'd planned things: my goals, my future, my life.

This place where I'd made out with Celia a few times beneath a blacklight, trying to explain its value, while skirting its significance. I wished I could've made love to her amid its purple glow, but that was not meant to be.

I was leaving this. I was being asked---no *told*---to sever ties with the space in which I'd discovered myself. It didn't even look the same anymore. This was no longer my place.

I finished packing my bag for the plane. I listened for the phone, but it never rang. I looked at the clock. It was approaching noon and we needed to be on the road by 12:30PM. *Just a few more things to do.*

I thought about Celia. I knew she'd be at the airport and I couldn't wait to see her. It had been too long.

I smiled when I thought about her being pregnant. I couldn't wrap my head around it: *we were having a baby!* Celia wanted a girl---someone she could promise a real childhood to. I wanted a boy---someone to carry on my bloodline. Really, it didn't matter. It would be a beautiful child. I couldn't wait to see Celia today and touch her, kiss her and rub her belly.

My dad knocked on the door. He popped his head in before I could answer.

"Got your stuff around?" He asked.

"Yeah. I'm set," I said.

My dad opened the door and my room seemed to get brighter. It was odd.

"Say goodbye to what you used to know, Rollie," he said. "You're stepping out into a whole, new world." He had a smile on his face that I couldn't discern. Was it pride in me, or was it mockery? I didn't ask. I didn't want to know.

I took one last peek into my room before I pulled the door shut. It was like closing my own coffin lid. My old life was dead. The carefree, ne'er-do-well, impervious days of high school were gone. My gas-pumping, car-washing, auto slave job at the dealership was gone. My car and all the memories made within it? Way gone---my dad sold it to the highest bidder and split the cash with me. The parental control thing? Sort of gone. My love life and my future? *Who the hell knows?*

I sat in the back of my mom's car as we made our way to the airport. It was a quiet drive. I didn't know what to think. I was leaving. I was going away to school, yet I felt like I was being taken to prison. *No conversing with the inmate.* All communication will be avoided. It is a felony to interact in any way with the inmate... *fuck this.*

"Mom, did Uncle Rich get my stuff yet?" I asked, breaking the silence.

"Not that I know of, dear. Probably after you get there," my mom responded.

"I hope so. The less I have to worry about, the better."

"Your Uncle Richard will make sure your things are fine, don't fret."

"I know, it's just a bit nerve-racking, that's all. There's a lot to think about."

It was silent again. This drive to the airport was longer than any other. It seemed to take forever. I was trying to psych myself up to see Celia. She would be there---I just knew it. *I'm sorry God for doubting you before, but please, do what you can to make sure that Celia comes to see me---I miss her and love her so much. I know you know how much I love her. We're going to have a baby! Please bring her to me. Please, Oh Lord. Amen.*

My dad drove into the airport parking lot, found a spot and parked. We sat in the car for a moment before we got out.

"It seems odd to bring this up, since we're here and all. But where are Jerry and Devon?" I asked. "Why didn't they come with us?"

"They're going to meet us later," my mom said. Her face was beaming. "Your brother had something to do last minute. He said it was a surprise."

"A surprise?! What could it be?" I wondered aloud.

"Well, we can't tell you. We don't want to spoil it," she stated.

I was hoping---with my last, frayed string of hope---that the 'surprise' my older brother had was Celia. I was hoping that he'd called her, picked her up and was bringing her here. That would be the best gift ever!

"I don't want to say anything, but you're going to love it! That's all---I've said too much!" My mom happily blurted.

It is Celia! Way to go Jerry! I knew my brother would come through for me! Those were the thoughts that ran through my mind.

We entered the terminal, took care of the formalities with the ticket agent and went through security and to the gate. We found a place to sit and wait. I excused myself and went to look out the window.

I watched the grounds crew service the aircraft on the tarmac. I tried to imagine what the baggage handlers were saying as they mercilessly tossed suitcases into the bellies of the planes. They were all wearing sunglasses and some type of hearing protection as they wandered the tarmac in control of our safety, our destiny---and our luggage.

I turned around and scanned the gate area in the hopes I'd see Celia. She was not there, but I had to believe she'd be arriving at any moment.

My dad joined me and we talked about the planes. I told him how in a way, I'd wished I was travelling farther, so I could fly on a bigger aircraft. I missed the jumbo jets we used to ride when I was a kid. Our family vacations were far and wide and took us to so many great locations. Celia's family travelled a lot, too---but for completely different reasons and to less than favorable locales, I'm sure.

A Boeing 727 roared by and shook the windows. Thin puffs of black smoke poured out of the engines as the plane sped down the runway. It lifted off just beyond a wall. We could no longer see it. I wondered where it was going.

"Dad, I want to thank you for everything," I said, still looking out the window.

"What do you mean?" He asked.

"Just for being there and always making sure we were taken care of."

"That's kind of my job, Rollie."

"I know, but you seemed to do it better than other dads. We were always OK."

My dad seemed overwhelmed by my accolade.

"It wasn't too difficult. I just did what I knew best," he said. "There's no trick to being a good father, you just have to know the rights and wrongs. You'll make mistakes, but you learn from them and you atone."

I looked at my dad. "I hope that when I become a father, I can even be half the man you are," I said.

"You'll do fine. You still have a lot of life to live before that day comes," he said. "You've got to learn and grow a little; see and do things; find the man you want to be." He put his hand on my shoulder. "Don't rush anything, Rollie. You're still young."

I only wish that were true.

My dad and I walked back and sat with my mom. My brother and sister still had not arrived---neither had Celia. My mom smiled and asked me if I was ready for my trip.

"I suppose so," I said. "I don't have much of a choice, now, right?"

"You're going to do fine, Roland," my mom stated. "You're so nervous about change and unfamiliar things, but they're good. New things are OK. Trust me."

"I know, it's just…"

"You're worried about meeting new people and what to expect, I know."

Actually, that wasn't even close to what I was thinking, but OK.

"Yeah, I guess that's it," I relented. "Remember how long it took me to assimilate to our new house."

"I do! That did take some time," my mom said.

"I suppose it's like that, just on a bigger, *more collegiate,* scale."

My mom chuckled at my comment. She looked around the terminal.

"I wonder where your brother and sister are," she said. "They should've been here by now."

"I know. I'm going to be leaving real soon," I said. "This 'surprise' better be worth it." My words were sprinkled with a hint of sarcasm.

No sooner had we discussed my sibling's whereabouts and they showed up. Jerry was carrying a flat, square box that looked like a stack of records. Devon strolled beside him with an impish grin on her face. Celia was not with them. I could feel my heart sink and I felt slightly sick. I knew I was not going to see her today. I would be leaving without kissing my true love, my fiancée---the mother of my child---goodbye. I was crushed.

"Hey guys, sorry we're so late," Jerry said. "There was a crazy accident near the new freeway."

"Well, I guess we need to find a different way home from here," my mom mused.

My dad concurred. "Yeah, it'll be nice when they get that road finished," he said. "There's too much confusion in that construction zone."

I didn't care. I just wanted to die right now. I didn't want to be anywhere but in Celia's arms and that was beyond possibility. Jerry handed me the box he was carrying and told me to open it.

"What is it?" I asked.

"You have to open it!" Devon exclaimed. "It's really cool! You'll love it!"

She was overly excited about the gift. I didn't want to stifle her enthusiasm or disappoint her. God knows I was disappointed enough for us all.

I opened the box and inside was a layer of crepe tissue paper. Underneath was a book. It was not just any book; however, it was a handmade picture book.

I opened the front cover to a collection of random pictures of me and my family from over the years. There were pictures from vacations; shots of us attempting to fish; everyone dolled up in their travel clothes; our old camper. There were baby pictures and embarrassing kid photos---the kind your folks seem to magically find when you start dating. There were also clippings from newspapers and magazines; articles and ephemera from places we'd been, shows we'd seen and a hodgepodge of other things I hadn't seen in years.

The book was great. It made me wish I wasn't leaving my family. It made me cry. For the first time in a while, I was crying over something that was not Celia. It made me wonder: why do you get these kinds of gifts when you're going far away, or being separated? Why does such a loving gesture have to be so hard to take?

"Dude, are you OK?" Devon asked.

"Yeah, Dev. I'm just fine," I said. "This is an amazing gift. Thank you, guys, so much!" I got up to give everyone a hug.

"We knew you'd love it. Wait till you get a chance to really check it out," Jerry said. "There's so many crazy pics in there---a lot of stuff I didn't even remember!"

"Now, *Mister Pisster Pessimist,* wasn't that worth the wait?" My mom chided.

"It was for sure, mom," I said. "I can't wait to see the rest of it and read the clippings."

The gate agent announced my flight would be boarding in fifteen minutes. Fifteen minutes---*a quarter of an hour.* That was all I had left of the life I'd known. It was not a lot of time, but it was enough time for Celia to get here.

I peered toward the hall to see if she was walking toward my gate, but she was not. She was nowhere to be seen. I wanted to ask my brother if he had one more surprise for me, but I knew he didn't. I would have to wait until November to see Celia. The time between now and November was a hell of a lot longer than fifteen minutes. I gave up hope on today. I wondered why she was not here. I felt so empty.

It was time to get on the plane. My mom, my sister and I got the waterworks flowing. My dad and my brother were feeling the same but held back their emotions---as all good men do. I was not a good man. Right now---I was nothing.

I hugged everyone, said goodbye and walked toward the jet way. I moved between the seats and around the bags on the floor. I found a spot in line and inched my way up to the gate agent. She took my ticket and I stepped through the jet way door. I never looked back.

The smell of jet fuel and the blast of heat inside the jet way were accentuated on this August day. I closed my eyes for a second, opened them and continued to the plane.

I stepped aboard and was greeted by a cute stewardess who smelled of Chantilly. I could feel my eyes begin to well with tears. I returned her greeting and moved down the aisle to my seat. I tucked in by the window and put the gift box and my bag under the seat in front of me. I buckled my seatbelt and looked out the window.

I was facing opposite of where my family would be. They would stay until my flight left. We would not see each other.

I put my hands to my face and began to cry. I had so many things to lose it over and couldn't pick just one. I let them all flow out of me.

At this moment, in this seat and on this airplane, the old version of Roland Jacob McCallum ceased to exist. A new version would take his place and I wasn't sure how to deal with that. The old version knew things. The old version had family and friends close by. The old version had a decent job. The old version liked to have fun but could be serious when he had to be. The old version had a handle on things---at least as good of a handle as an eighteen-year-old could have. More than anything; however, the old version had Celia.

BOOK TWO

CHAPTER 18

I'd been at school for a month and half and hated every minute of it. I'd made a few friends but stayed to myself most of the time. The classes were terrible, and the teachers were even worse. Looking back, the Air Force may have been a better option.

I wrote Celia just about every day. If I wasn't writing to her, I was thinking about her. I'd called her a few times as well. I made her a tape with some new songs I'd been listening to and a few of her favorites. In between the songs I chatted. I talked about this and that, while playing DJ and introducing the songs I figured she didn't know. I thought it was the best gift I could give her. She got to hear my voice and how much I was missing her---and the songs to prove it.

Every day I would go to the mailbox and it was always a gamble whether I was going to return happy or not. Today was a happy day. I got two letters from Celia. I couldn't wait to read them.

I sat in the common area and opened one of the letters. I could smell Celia's perfume on the paper. I breathed her spritzed scent and it made me swoon. I haven't smelled her in such a long time, and this was like taking of a shot of whisky, or a hit off a joint---I could feel the buzz right away.

I read Celia's words and even though they were lovely and sentimental, there was a slight tinge of disconnect in them. I couldn't figure out why. Maybe it was just my imagination? I read the letter again. The strange feeling of uncertainty I had waned as I followed the curve of her script a second time. Everything was OK. She still loved me, and I loved her more than ever. I chose to wait and read the second letter later.

That night, I was in bed with a flashlight and I opened the other letter. Again, the aroma of Chantilly encircled me as it delicately flowed from the paper. I was entranced. My uplifted demeanor would be short-lived.

As I read what Celia had written, it made little sense. Earlier in the day, I'd had the same problem, but I'd re-read the letter and it was OK. Not this time. This time things seemed to fall further away with each read. What the hell? She'd written the letters within a day of each other, but I couldn't figure out why they were so different. After a while, the words became incoherent. The letters became vague symbols and meant absolutely nothing. Maybe I was just tired. I hope that's all it was.

A couple of weeks went by since I'd received those two letters from my true love. After that, there was nothing else--- not even a postcard. I'd tried to call her several times, but the line was busy, or no one answered. I was worried. I was wondering what was going on, why she hadn't written, and why I couldn't get a call through.

I had exams coming up in a few days. I tried to look at this *correspondence hiatus* as a good thing. I needed to concentrate on my work. I was failing a few of my classes and was about to be put on academic probation. I wanted to avoid this. However, the more I tried to *not* think about Celia, the more prominent she was in my mind.

I couldn't sleep at night and to try, I started hitting the bottles of alcohol my roommate Brett had stashed in our closet. During study times, I took swigs of everything I could find. Some mornings I'd wake up sick or hungover; other mornings I'd wake up late and blow off class. I just didn't care anymore.

I gave up on the idea that not hearing from Celia was good. I gave up on studying. I failed all my exams and got put on academic probation. I was a wreck and I didn't care about anything except Celia---and now I was wondering about our baby.

On the weekend after exams I called Celia again. This time we talked.

"Hello?" A very longed-for voice answered.

"Hi, baby it's me!" I said, sounding like an excited child.

"Hey, you. What's going on?" Celia asked.

"Nothing. I just hadn't heard from you in such a long time. Are you OK?"

"I've been better."

"Are you sick? What's wrong?"

"Just... stuff. You know. It's always something."

I didn't know. I had no idea.

"I hate being away from you," I said.

"Me, too---I told you not to go," she said coldly.

"I know. Let's not talk about that, OK?"

"OK."

I took a deep breath. "Are you alone?" I asked.

"I could be. Why?" She wondered aloud.

"I have to ask you something that's... well... something we haven't talked about."

"What?"

"The baby," I whispered. "How's the baby?"

There was silence on the other end of the line. I hadn't heard a click. I knew she was still there.

"Celia? Honey?"

"I'm here."

"Did you hear what I said?"

"I love you. I have to go."

Now, there was a click---and a dial tone. She was gone and I was left alone in the phone booth clutching the handset with one hand, while trying to scrape up my heart with the other.

I hung up the phone and went back to my room. The hall seemed longer and eerily brighter the further I walked. The blood drained from my face. I was cold and pale; my hands were heavy and numb. I walked in my room and fell into a heap in the large chair by the door and wept. I don't know what just happened. I could feel my soul being ripped out of my body. I needed to get out of here. I needed to go home.

Brett came in a saw me in a shamble. I was inconsolable. He tried to help, but nothing he said was working, nor was it what I wanted to hear.

"Man, chicks. They're always so complicated," he said. "I got a girl back home too. I never know from week to week what I'm gonna' get."

I tried to wave off him and his testosterone-fueled pep talk.

"No, man, you gotta' listen to me," he said. "It'll be fine. You two will fix all of this. You will."

I stared at him. "Leave me alone, OK?" I said. "You don't know what's up. It's more than just my girl. There are so many other things. I just want to be by myself."

"No. I can't do that. You're hurting and you need to chill," Brett said. "I've seen you bad before, but this is the worst. I'll get you a drink. What do you want?"

He pulled out four bottles of stuff and handed them to me. I didn't turn any of them down. I gulped down what I could from one and passed it back for another. Within half an hour, I was blitzed. I remembered what was happening, but my command of the English Language had deteriorated.

I held up a finger and gave Brett the 'drunk wag.'

"Lissinman... I love my *feeyasay,* you know?" I slurred. "I called her... shesaidshe..."

"What did she say?" Brett asked.

I squinted and my voice became a whisper. "Shesezshees..."

"What?" He asked. "She says she's what?"

"Shesezshespregnin... *andismine,* you know?" I whispered. I moved closer to his face, as I pulled on his shirt. "Imgonnbeyadad! Canyoubleedat?" Me... adad?! Fugginnutstha'shit, man."

"Whoa! Rollie! That is so cool!" Brett said. "I didn't know your girl was pregnant."

"Buhcheh... checkitman... she wuntell me aboudit. *Wheresmyfugginkid?* Mygirlzname... ya... yaknow'er name, right?" I sloppily asked.

"It's *Celia,* right?" Brett inquired.

"YEAH! Seeeee-llll-yaaaa! Fuggin-eh right. Satsmylove... *SMYBABE!*" I yelled. I started to lose my energy. I felt weak and began to drift.

I closed my eyes and even though I was not asleep, I heard myself snore. I jolted and looked around. Brett was still talking, but I couldn't make out anything he was saying. I slowly and clumsily smacked the arm of the chair.

"Sleepswotineedadoo, *Big Bee.* Eye... yeah... Gottagess gessumsleep." I told him---barely.

Brett covered me up and I heard the door shut. He'd finally left me alone like I'd asked, but now more than ever I needed someone around.

I started crying and blubbering. I wept alone in my room, far from everything I'd known. I was so broken. I was so unsure of what was going on. Again, I just wanted to go home.

I woke up late the next morning still in the chair. It was Sunday and the halls were quiet. Most of the dorm was probably still sleeping off benders from the night before. Surprisingly, I was OK---a little sloshy, but OK.

I remembered most of my rant and felt embarrassed. I peered around and didn't see my roommate. I felt my face and head to make sure nothing had been shaved off me while I was passed out.

I was slow to get up, but once I got mobile, I was fine. I stunk. I smelled like cheap liquor and bad taco meat with an odd finish of secondhand smoke. My mouth tasted like a rancid steak and my ass---*just my ass*---was sweaty.

I folded the blanket and placed it on the back of the chair. I needed to clean up. I got my things for a shower and went into the bathroom. On the desk I spied a huge stogie. Beneath it was an index card. Curiosity got the best of me and I picked up the card and read it.

Congratulations Rollie---you're going to
be one hell of a father! Big B.

I smiled and my eyes welled a little. What a grand gesture. I hardly knew this guy.

After my shower I got dressed and went to call my parents. I hadn't talked to them in a while. They'd already received notice of my academic probation; it was time to stand tall and face the firing squad.

My mom answered the phone and sounded ecstatic to hear from me. She did not let me forget that I'd been neglectful in the communications department.

"Roland! What a nice surprise! Do you need money?" My mom asked. I could hear her smile through her cynicism.

"No money, mom," I said. "I just... I just feel bad I haven't called. It's been really hard for me all around."

"It's OK. Your dad and I understand how difficult it is for you being so far away."

"How is everyone?"

"We're all great. Your dad's been busy---there's a new aircraft engine being designed, and you know how he is---got to be the first in," She said, touting my father's achievements.

My mom expounded. "Jerry's been working on a critical paper about the use of chemical weapons in World War I---it's really good! Devon is doing well in school and she's going to be trying out for the marching band. That French horn is finally going to get some use."

"That's terrific! How are *you,* doing?" I asked.

"Oh, you know. New school year---so many things to do. There's always those *special* years," my mom said. She sounded proud. "My new students are fabulous---in fact, I think you know one of them: Ricky Chandler?"

Hearing that name caused me to stir. "That's cool. Speaking of Ricky... how is Celia?" I asked. "Have you guys seen her lately?"

"Have *you* talked to her?" My mom asked coldly.

"Yeah, yesterday---and it was really weird," I responded.

"There's something not right with that family, Roland. Celia's a good girl and all, but there's something unsettling going on under that roof."

I didn't understand. "'Unsettling'? Like what?" I asked.

"I'm not sure," my mom said. "I really can't say anything else."

This was freaking me out. I tried to subtly press for more information.

"I just wondered if you've seen her," I said. "I know she liked coming to see Devon, maybe they've gotten a chance to talk."

"No. We haven't seen her much," my mom said. "We ran into her at the store a couple of times, but that's about it. I know you miss her."

"Oh, mom, I do. I miss her so much. I hardly hear from her and when I do it's... I don't know."

"Well, you'll be seeing her soon enough. November is not too far away."

I felt a little better. I needed that ray of sunshine, because now I had to discuss my failing grades.

"Um, have you and dad gotten any letters from the school?" I asked timidly.

"Yes. We have," my mom retorted. "We've decided to wait till you're home to discuss them. This is not a *phone conversation*."

"Fair enough. It'll give me time to prepare," I said, breathing a sigh of relief.

My mom's voice sounded cheery again. "Would you like to talk to your father or anyone else?" She asked.

"Can I talk to dad really fast?" I asked.

"Yep. Here he is."

I heard my mom cup the mouthpiece. The unintelligible mumblings sounded like something out of *Peanuts*.

My dad got on the line and sounded jovial. "Hey! Rollie," he said. "What's happening? How's everything?"

I wanted to be honest. I wanted to say: *you've seen the letters.* I wanted to tell him how much I hate it here, but my dad was in such a good mood I was not going to spoil it.

"Things are OK, dad. How about you?" I asked. "Mom says you've got a new engine design in the works." I eagerly awaited one of my dad's blunt and succinct descriptions of the new equipment.

"It's pretty high-tech. We're going to be using *composites*," he said. "I'm not entirely sure of what composites are, but they're changing how we fly. It's supposed to be really lightweight and more fuel efficient than anything out there. They're going to test the new engine in our shop and then after it passes, McDonnell Douglas may consider it for the new DC-10 models. Pretty cool stuff!"

Wow. And I was expecting: 'I'm testing an engine...'

I had to tip my proverbial cap to my dad: he was embracing change and the unfamiliar; getting with the times and looking fearlessly toward the future. I was still hesitant of it all. Change scared me. Change within my relationship with Celia scared me the most.

"That's great, dad!" I said, coming back to the conversation.

"You know, you've only got a few weeks until you come home for break, are you looking forward to it?" My dad asked. He sounded like a coach.

"I am. I can't wait to see you guys" I said. "I really miss Celia, too. She's been on my mind a lot."

"Yeah. We haven't seen much of her, but your mom has her brother in her class---kid's name is...? Um...?"

"Ricky," I interjected.

"Yeah, *Ricky*," my dad said.

I didn't want to talk anymore. My head was beginning to ache. I needed to go and clear my mind. Moreover, I needed some answers.

"Dad, hey... I've got to get going," I said. "There's a couple of people that have been waiting---very patiently---for the phone and I've..." I paused. "I'll get some letters out to you all, some pictures too. Tell Jerry and Devon I'm sorry I missed talking to them, OK?"

I lied about the callers, but not about missing my siblings.

"OK, Rollie. Listen---try to keep your head in the class-room, ya' hear?" My dad said. "Stay out of trouble and we'll see you real soon."

"I love you dad. Tell mom, Jerry and Dev I love them too, alright."

"You bet. Talk to you later, Rollie. Goodbye."

"Bye, dad."

I hung up and dug another two dollars and seventy-five cents in coins out of my tin and tried to call Celia. All the talk about her made me want to hear her voice. The things my mother said sent a chill down my spine. What could be so 'un-settling going on under that roof'? I had to know. At the very least, I just had to tell Celia I loved her.

Her phone rang and rang. Five rings and I hung up. I slammed the handset down and all my coins poured out of the phone. It was like a slot machine pay out; except I was losing.

I gave up after about ten tries. By now, there truly was someone who wanted the phone. I stepped out.

CHAPTER 19

In the next few weeks I'd gotten a couple of scattered letters from Celia, but not much more. It was as if she'd started them, forgotten to finish them, but sent them anyway. There was a definite theme with her letters: the less of them she wrote, the more mysterious they became. One day they just stopped. I kept writing. She did not. I was devastated. I didn't understand what was happening. I just knew I needed to see her.

I'd tried to call few times. Each time I did, there would be some issue: the phone would just ring and ring, I'd get a busy signal, or there was a message the line was 'being checked for trouble.' I finally stopped calling. I was distraught. I was missing my girl. I was missing my love.

November finally rolled around and it was time for our first long break. My folks had deposited money into my account so I could buy a plane ticket home. I was looking forward to seeing everyone---especially Celia, but I didn't know if that was a possibility. I weighed my options. I debated and I finally decided that even though I wanted to come home, I would forego this break in favor of the next one in December. It was the Christmas/ midterm break. It was longer and had much more significance than the November break. It was only three weeks away. I could ride the storm out until them.

Since I was getting no replies from Celia, I was able to clear my head and actually study. I wasn't dissing her, but I wasn't making a concerted effort to write her lengthy novellas professing my love, either. I'd dropped a line or two, but that was about it. I certainly hadn't moved on---there was no way.

Instead, I just decided to give her some space and time. I could flourish academically and still continue my relationship. It was all I could do for the moment.

I sat at my desk one day in December. It was just a couple days before the break. I was working diligently on a project. *Working diligently*---something I hadn't done the entire time I'd been on this campus. I needed to finish. I had a deadline to meet and was sweating through all the bullshit that went with deadlines.

I was completing one of the best projects I'd ever done. I'd conceptualized, designed, created and was about to present the next big move in breakfast. I was taking the Kellogg's *Corn Flakes* box to another dimension. Simple, innocent and pure corn flakes given a new life and purpose. I hated them growing up---only lots of sugar could convince me to eat them. However, this box---*my design*---was out to make kids love this cereal and embrace it for the iconic brand that it is. Forget the sugar--- the *box* is sweet. This cereal is good---you know you want it! I needed to step away from my work for a minute.

Brett yelled out 'mail call,' and dropped a pile of postmarked documents on my desk. It was exactly the respite I was in search of. I filed through the mail, seeking something I'd been desperately wanting: a letter from Celia. I was going home in a couple of days and I couldn't wait to see her again. Photographs and dreams cannot replace the real thing.

As I thought about her, I sensed I could smell her perfume and feel her skin. I could hear her voice so clearly. I closed my eyes and let the sensations engulf me. I smiled as I thought about how it was going to be to see her. My smile got bigger as I thought about how wonderful it was going to be to kiss her again. I sighed softly when the thought of making love with her arose in my mind. I missed making love, but I missed holding her hand just as much. More than anything---I just missed *her*.

Bills, letters to rush frats, a couple of letters from my sister and a postcard from my brother; a flyer inviting me and 'a friend' to a new pizza joint near campus; a mailer about up-coming activities for next semester---that was all I found in this collection of correspondence. I shook my head in defeat. I read the stuff from my siblings and trashed the rest of it. I felt completely empty and lost.

Why hadn't I heard from Celia? What had happened to us? Didn't she love me anymore? If she didn't, why couldn't she tell me so? Maybe she was gearing up for my visit and didn't want to ruin things she'd planned. *Was I supposed to believe that?* She was so sporadic with her letters already---both in content and frequency---that her not writing because of some great surprise planned for my homecoming seemed too ridiculous to even contemplate.

I'm an idiot.

"Yo, B. Is this all the mail I got?" I asked.

"Yep, Rollie, that's it," Brett said. "There's a lot there. Expecting something else?"

"Yeah, but it's no big deal," I lamented.

Brett cracked open a beer and offered me one. I thought about passing, but it sounded good and I took it.

"Thanks, man," I said. "I can use this."

"You looking forward to seeing your family over break?" Brett asked. "I'll bet you're *totally* looking forward to seeing your fiancée. How's that going?"

"I am really looking forward to seeing my family, man," I told him. "As for Celia, I'm not sure what's going on there. It's been weird. That's why I was asking about the mail. I thought maybe I'd hear from her."

Brett shook his head. "That's so messed up. She's pregnant, right?" He asked. "You guys are engaged, why the lousy communication?"

"I don't know," I said.

My response was two-fold. I didn't know why the communication was so lousy and I wasn't sure anymore if she was actually pregnant.

"I guess I'll figure it all out when I get home, eh?" I said.

"Yeah. That's all you can do." Brett said, with a sigh.

CHAPTER 20

The day I left to go home it snowed lightly. The sun was out in patches, but it did little to warm the temperature. Brett drove us to the airport. He was flying out to visit his parents in Wisconsin. I was quiet for most of the drive. I didn't know what to say about anything. The discussions we had were mostly small talk. We mentioned family sporadically. I didn't mention Celia at all. I watched the snow. It squalled at one point and made it difficult to see the road. I couldn't wait to get to the airport. I couldn't wait to get home.

We arrived and parked and took a bus to the terminal. There were three other people aboard: a young woman and her two little kids. One of the kids kept staring at me. She was pale with auburn hair and hazel eyes. I tried not to look at her, but no matter where I turned my head, I knew she was looking at me. I could see her no matter what. She looked like Celia as a little girl. I began to imagine that this girl was what Celia became while she was on the swings. I closed my eyes and took a deep breath. I was trying to hold back my tears as my mind played images of the little girl on the swings at the park. I finally looked at her. She saw my red eyes and said something to her mother about boys not crying. This boy was definitely not upholding that myth.

The bus stopped. We all got off and dispersed to our respective airline counters to check in. The mother and her kids went in an opposite direction from Brett and me. The little girl continued staring at me. I waved to her subtly. She blushed and turned away quickly.

I checked in and put my bag on the scales to be weighed. The ticket agent saw the weight but pulled at the bag like it was going to be heavy. She nearly threw it across the terminal, as if she was competing in an Olympic hammer throw. I laughed and she saw me. Her face reddened with embarrassment, but she started laughing, too.

"Next time I'll believe the scales," she said, rolling her eyes.

"It is a big bag," I said. "Anyone could've made the mistake."

She continued to blush and smiled. "You're too cute," she said. "Glad no one else saw that."

I smiled back at the ticket agent as she handed my boarding passes to me. Her suitcase gaffe was the highlight of my day so far.

I went through security and looked to around to find my gate.

Brett and I met up at the airport food court and grabbed sandwiches from a little cafeteria. The place was cheap. Cheap was good. We're college students. We're broke.

We found a table and sat down to eat. Brett got an egg salad on white. I got a ham and cheese on rye with light mayonnaise, a big, crisp piece of lettuce and thin slices of tomato--- just like the sandwiches Celia made for me when I worked on the school newspaper.

"You ready for your flight?" Brett asked between bites.

"Yeah. You?" I inquired.

"Dude, I just want to bail out and forget about that tuition-financed prison for a while," Brett said. "I've got to clear my head, you know?"

I nodded. "Absolutely," I said. "I'm hoping to have a nice Christmas; spend time with the 'rents; harass my brother; take my sister shopping, but most of all I just want to see Celia."

"I know you miss her a ton," Brett said.

"More than you can imagine," I said. I leaned in so the others seated around us couldn't hear me. "I just want to take her to bed and make love to her for the next two weeks."

Brett got a puzzled look on his face. "She's pregnant, isn't she?" He asked.

I dropped my head. "I gotta' be honest, man. I don't even know anymore," I said.

He gave me a contemplative scowl. "Wait... I thought..." he said.

I cut him off. "Yeah, so did I," I said. "I have to take you back a bit. Maybe you can piece it together."

"I'll see what I can do," he said with a smile.

"On grad night, we had sex for the first time," I explained. "We did it twice. Once with a rubber and once without in the shower; that time, I pulled out. Things got weird after that. We were up and down. Then we had sex again a couple of weeks before I left to come here. *That* was something."

"Go on..." Brett said, quite intrigued.

"Anyway, we're outside kissing and the next thing I know, she's asking to give me a blowjob right outside of her house---in public," I said. My voice lowered to almost silent.

"No way!" Brett said with a gasp.

"Yeah! This is my girl Celia, here," I said. "When I met her, it took forever for her to let me kiss her, then we make love the first time and she turns into a nympho."

Brett shook his head. "Man," he said. "Well, continue."

"OK, so we do the oral thing and she was crazy," I said. "I don't even know how else to describe it. Then she says asks me to make love to her..."

Brett interjected, "Outside of her house?"

"No, no... she wanted to," I said. "But we got in my car. Sorry, I left that out."

"I was gonna' say..."

"Yeah, so there we are, in the backseat of my ride and we're having sex again. I didn't have a rubber this time and at first, I tried to resist, but she... I couldn't say no. We do it---without protection---and I tell her I want to stop. I was about to come, and she leans up to me and says: 'I want you to get me pregnant.'"

Brett sat back. "Whoa! That's wild!" He said.

"That's one way of putting it!" I responded.

"So, what happened after you guys fucked in the car?"

"Well, not much. I called her and it was anybody's guess if she would be home or even talk to me. When I did talk to her it was distant. She said all the right things, but they didn't sound sincere. I couldn't get my head around it.

"The night before I left to come to school, I called her, and she said she'd see me at the airport. She never showed."

"That's messed up."

"Totally. What's worse is the fact that I haven't seen her since the last night we had sex."

"Dude, that is so uncool," Brett said. He scowled again and shook his head.

"That's what happened. So yeah, that's why I'm not sure if she's pregnant or not," I said. "If she is, she's close to five months along. I want to believe that she is. I want that so much."

I looked at my half-eaten sandwich. I lost my appetite.

Brett put his hands together like he was praying. He tapped his hands to his chin and closed his eyes.

"Rollie, I really hope this trip brings you what you want," he said. "I hope you get the answers you're seeking. I hope you and Celia find each other and the love and happiness you talk about.

"You totally love this chick. I've never met anyone who's loved a girl so much before. I'll pray for you, man. I want to see you get your 'happily ever after.'"

"Thank you, B," I said. "You have no idea what that means to me."

I heard my flight being called for boarding. I shook Brett's hand and told him I'd see him in a couple of weeks.

"Safe travels, dude," he said.

"Same to you," I replied.

There had been music playing in the terminal, but neither of us paid much attention to it. Paul McCartney's odd ditty 'Wonderful Christmastime' began to play. I pointed to the speakers above us.

"I wish you this," I said. "But better than the song."

Brett laughed. "Yeah, it's not one of his best," he said.

"Not at all, but it's a classic. You have to love it."

"Yeah. You kinda' do."

I headed to the gate. On my way I spotted a small bookstore. I had a minute, so I went in. I wanted to read something to help take my mind off everything. I found a paperback copy of Ernest Hemingway's *The Sun Also Rises*. The cover was colorful and vibrant; beautiful but obscure. Upon closer viewing, I discerned the artwork; it was a bullfight mid-scene. I didn't even read a line. I just bought the book. The title and the cover image were enough to convince me I needed this book. I wanted to read it. It was going to take me away from my problems---at least for a little while.

The final call for my flight was announced. I hurriedly paid for the book, ran to my gate and got in line. I looked out the window as I moved up the queue. The snow seemed to be falling harder. I began to wonder if my flight would be delayed or cancelled. That could not happen. I had to get out of here. I had to make my connection in Chicago and get home.

I smiled at the gate agent as she took my boarding pass. She bid me a nice flight and I boarded the plane. *Thank God.*

I took my seat and looked out the window. The snow was swirling in pyramids and it was getting dark out. The tall lights along the tarmac began to come on. I watched the snow spiral close to the soft glow emitting from the mercury vapor bulbs. The snowflakes looked like glass moths as they spun and danced in the light beams. The beams were becoming brighter and longer as the sky got darker.

The captain announced we were pushing back. I heaved a sigh and smiled. We wouldn't be delayed or cancelled today. In an hour, I would be in Chicago awaiting my next flight---the flight that would take me home. I took my new book out of the bag and began to read as we taxied down the runway.

CHAPTER 21

We arrived in Chicago and it was an hour earlier. I had an hour and a half layover here only to return to the same time zone I'd just left. It was stupid and confusing. I read my book and dismissed the formalities.

I found myself becoming enthralled with what I was reading. I was relating to characters and their tense situations and relationships; sympathizing with some, while cursing others. *Jake Barnes* and I were kindred spirits at the moment: impotent, away from home; unsure of our futures and moreover---our loves. I'd never felt so akin to literature. I closed the book for a moment and looked at the cover. I was anticipating that bright, colorful imagery. I had to continue.

My flight was announced, and I did not hesitate to board when my row was called. I figured the quicker I got on, the quicker I'd be home. I shuffled down the aisle and gazed about at the bleary-eyed travelers. They all seemed lost. They looked as if they hadn't slept for days and were not sure why they were here. I know I looked the same to them.

Toward the back of the plane I could hear a baby cry. It was the cry of a newborn: strange and primal; desperate and unknown. I didn't want to sit close to the baby. I was not averse to its crying; I just didn't want to look at a newborn. My eyes glazed as I thought about the baby---*mine and Celia's baby,* and if that was a reality I'd be going home to.

I found my seat. It was close to the new mother and her infant. I stowed my bag and put my book in the seat pocket. While the space next to me was still unoccupied, I got up and went to the bathroom to get a cup of water. While only moments ago I didn't want to see the baby, I suddenly found myself intrigued and glanced at it quickly on my way to the bathroom. When I was returning to my seat, I stopped.

"Pardon me, but can I have a peek at the baby?" I asked the mother.

The mother seemed happily surprised. "Sure!" She said. "His name is Aaron. He's a little fussy."

She pulled back the blanket so I could see his tiny face.

"Oh my God! What a little angel," I said, as my face beamed. "How old is he?"

"Just a couple weeks," she said. "I didn't want to travel with a newborn, because of... well... the obvious, but what do you do, right?"

"He's so little," I said.

His eyes were closed, and his tiny lip sneered. A little shock of black hair poked from the top of his swaddling blanket.

"He looks like Elvis, a bit," I commented. "The hair---got the lip thing going."

The mother chuckled. "I didn't see that!"

"You named him Aaron---that was the King's middle name. He's got royal blood."

"Oh my gosh! I didn't realize that, either."

"*Uh-huh*," I said, attempting a bad impersonation of Elvis Presley.

The mother laughed out loud and woke the baby slightly. He opened his big, blue eyes and let out a small cry. His eyes closed again. He seemed to calm down and go back to sleep.

"Thank you for letting me see him," I said.

"You're so welcome," the mother said. She covered tiny Aaron up again and lifted him to her shoulder. She softly patted his back and hummed a quiet song to him.

I passed the person who was sitting next to the new mother and when he saw his seatmate, he was not happy. He rolled his eyes and gave a scowl. The mother did not see it.

As soon as we were airborne, I read again. I returned to the stressed condition of Mr. Barnes and his compatriots as they made their way between Paris, France and Pamplona, Spain; their fights, their drinking and their love affairs. The affairs were especially engrossing. I felt both sympathetic and ashamed for the characters as they moved through their days with uncertainty, tension and contempt. I'd related before, but now I felt like I was in the story. I was still longing for the bright kaleidoscope the cover had promised.

The man next to me was snoring. The person in front of me leaned their seat so far back I could see the top of their head. I peered around and it seemed as if the entire plane was asleep. I continued reading.

When I got to the chapters featuring the *Festival of San Fermín* I was treated to the frenzy and fanfare I'd craved. My grandparents used to talk about their trip to Spain. My grandmother had a beautiful painting of a bullfight that I'd always loved. When I listened to them talk about the trip, I'd close my eyes and imagine it. I pictured a world of colorful fabrics and traditional Spanish headwear. I could smell the aromas of delicious food filling the air. I heard people singing songs and saw them dancing. They hugged and kissed as they celebrated in the warm, Spanish sun. Hemingway had described it just as my grandparents did; fifty years before they'd ever gone. Now as I read the words, I felt like I was there, too. I was in Pamplona caught up in the revelry and running with the bulls.

The pilot announced our pending arrival and I was no longer in Spain. I was seated next to an angry man who'd just been rousted from slumber. I was seated behind someone who I wanted to hit with my book. I was still on the airplane. I was only a few minutes from landing and barely an hour from my house. I put my book away. I was on my way home but had just been taken on a journey elsewhere. As we descended, I watched the lights of the towns and cars move beneath us. They were getting closer. *I was getting closer.* And the closer I got, the farther away I began to feel.

I took a deep breath and tried to relax. My anxiety increased as our altitude decreased. I looked out the window again and began to recognize lit landmarks and the curves of roads and streets. We crossed the berm which marked the end of the runway. The tires hit the ground and barked as the plane touched down. The engines screamed. The sound in the cabin was a heavy rumble. My head felt thick from the changes in air pressure. We were on the ground and moving toward the terminal.

I tried to fill my head with the idea that Celia would be here to meet me. She came to get me. She wanted to make up for not seeing me off. I couldn't wait to see her. I was looking forward to touching her belly as it swelled with our growing baby. I couldn't wait to kiss her lips and cheeks. I could feel her hand in mine as we walked through the terminal. I felt like the happiest man in the world.

The plane pulled to the jet way. In a flash the thoughts I'd had of Celia were gone. My mind went blank and my head hurt as my ears popped.

We came to a complete stop, and everyone began to get off the plane. People were bunched and crowded as they stood in the aisle. Some turned rudely and impatiently to other passengers; others pulled bags from the overheads and tried to be courteous. I remained seated. I wanted to wait until the line thinned. I wanted to be the last person off the plane.

The mother and her baby walked by as I sat. She was held up by the line, which had suddenly stopped moving.

"I was just wondering," she said. "Are you a father? You look so young."

"No. Well... not yet," I responded. I wanted to say more, but I didn't know any more than *maybe*.

"I was just so taken with your interest in my baby," she stated.

"I wanted to see if something so tiny could really make such a big sound," I said.

"He's got some lungs. Fortunately, he slept the whole flight."

"*You* won't get any sleep tonight!"

She laughed. "No, *my parents* won't get any sleep tonight," she said. "It's grandparent time!"

I laughed too. "You know they'll love it," I said.

The line began to move again.

With the exception of the crew, I was alone. I gathered my things and made my way off the plane. The stewardess at the door smiled, said 'goodbye' and bid me a happy holiday. I responded in kind before stepping into the jet way and into the real world.

It was warm for December. I hadn't noticed much snow when we landed. I entered the terminal and saw no one I recognized at first. I looked around and then I saw a lanky guy with close-cut brown hair standing next to my dad.

"Look at you, you, hippy freak!" My brother Jerry said as he and my dad walked up to me.

I shook my dad's hand. Jerry gave me a quick hug and apologized for his remark.

"It's cool. I guess what they chopped off you grew out of my scalp," I said as I mussed my hair.

My dad shook his head. "You should add 'haircut' to your Christmas list."

"It's winter. I had to grow it out for the warmth," I replied.

"They don't have barbers up there at school?" My dad asked smiling.

"Yeah, they're just not too good," I said as I pointed to my hair. "They stand too far away from the chair."

My dad chuckled. "Let's get your stuff and get home," he said.

I grabbed my suitcase off the carousel. My dad kept offering to carry it and I kept telling him no.

"I noticed how warm it is," I said. "It was snowing at school when I left earlier today."

"We've gotten a little, but not much to speak of, as you can see," my dad said.

Jerry commented, "I couldn't even get my skis out this

year."

"Skiing? Really?" I asked. "Your girlfriend get you into that?"

"Yeah. How'd you know?"

"You've just never been that adventurous. Is Hannah challenging your manhood?" I inquired with a laugh.

Jerry scowled and huffed, "No," he said. "We just wanted to try something new; some kind of winter activity."

"Yeah, but dude, skiing? It's totally dangerous. You could break your neck or something," I said with concern.

"Not if you know what you're doing."

"Olympic skiers have broken their necks."

"Well, maybe they weren't well trained."

I shook my head. "They're *freakin' Olympians,* dumb ass!" I exclaimed. "How more 'well trained' could they be?"

My dad interjected, "OK boys, this is not how we greet our siblings. You can fight about the dangers and attributes of skiing later."

"But dad..." Jerry blurted.

"Nope, sorry Jerr, but Rollie gets the last word on this."

I death stared at Jerry and stuck my tongue out at him behind his back.

Yeah, Rollie gets the last word on this.

We left the airport and headed for home. Everything looked so different. Once we'd gotten closer to town, I began to recognize things.

"Man, this place looks different at night," I said.

"Not much has changed," my dad stated.

We drove on and the ride seemed slow and long. Suddenly, my dad veered off and onto a ramp. We were travelling down a road I was really unfamiliar with.

"Dad, where are we going? Don't you usually take West drive to the parkway?" I asked.

"Nope. Not anymore," my dad said. "They opened the new freeway and it cuts about twenty minutes off the drive. It's great!" He sounded overly excited.

"Yeah, Rollie, it's a great drive," Jerry parroted.

I looked out the window as we sped down the new freeway. There was nothing to see except the occasional sign, light and passing car. It was nighttime, but there used to be things to see out this way. This was where U.S 27 used to run. Now there were no billboards; no little buildings; no gas station; no nothing---it was all gone.

I kept looking, hoping to see something. I found myself becoming distraught and lost.

"Dad, isn't this where U.S 27 used to be?" I asked.

My dad nodded. "Yes, it was. 27's gone now," he responded. "They closed the last bit of it just last week."

I shut my eyes for a second as tears began to fill them. I continued my road vigil and searched for anything recognizable. I looked for some type of sign. A sign that indicated the old road still had a breath of life. A sign that U.S 27 was not truly gone. I could find nothing.

The further we drove on the new road, the more I started to feel parts of my life disappearing. I had absolutely no idea where I was in relation to anything. The smooth humming of the pristine concrete beneath the tires of my dad's car was a sickening siren's song. It was singing to my soul. I sat empty, dejected and cold in the back of the car. I held on to a tiny, sinewy fiber of hope. However, it was something that I chose to not think about. I tucked it away and decided to wait until I had a clear head---and daylight, to deal with it.

We exited the freeway. Once again, I knew where I was. Even at night everything was instantly familiar. I named off shops, restaurants and random places in my head as we drove by.

"Recognize all this, Rollie?" My dad asked.

"Yeah, *this* looks familiar. There's a couple new places," I noted.

"It's amazing how things can change in such a short time, eh?"

"It sure is, dad. I feel like I've been gone for five years, not just five months."

"Well, if it's any consolation to you, things at home are pretty much the same--- just like you left them."

"That'll be nice," I responded. However, I knew full well that not *everything* was like I left it.

We got to the house and I felt a warm wave wash over me. My mom was standing in the door as we pulled into the driveway. My dad parked the car and the three of us got out. My dad opened the trunk and grabbed my suitcase. He commented on how light it was. I told him about the ticket agent, and he laughed.

My sister ran outside and grabbed me as I walked around the side of the car.

"Dude! You're home!" Devon shouted.

"Indeed I am. You got plans for me yet?" I asked.

"Oh, you know it!"

"Good. I need to keep busy while I'm here."

We walked to the door and my mom stepped out and gave me a hug.

"I'm so glad you're home, Roland," she said, squeezing me tight.

"It's good to be home, mom." I said.

"Look at you... what are they doing to you at that school?"

"Putting tonic on my hair and no decent food in my stomach. Is that what you were thinking, mom?"

"Something like that! Get in here! Let's get your things put away and... oh, there's so much to talk about," my mom said, as she ushered me into the house. It was the most scatterbrained I'd ever seen her.

It was so bright in the house. The entryway and kitchen looked so much more open than I remembered. Everything was so much bigger than it had been before---or so it seemed. Again, it was like five years rather than just five months.

My mom pointed me toward my room. I told her I remembered where it was. She started telling me where everything was. I already knew. That stuff hadn't changed a bit.

I opened the door to my room and was inundated with a brightness I wasn't expecting. The walls had been painted an even brighter white and the pictures I'd left up were now gone. Everything else was the same. The bed, the desk and the décor had not changed. I sat on my bed and rubbed the bedspread. I pushed the mattress a bit. It seemed firmer than I'd remembered. It hadn't changed. I'd just been sleeping on a lousy dorm mattress for the last few months.

I removed the pillows from their cases and looked at the tags. I wanted to make sure these were the same pillows that had been on the bed. One of them had a torn tag. That was the pillow Celia used when she and I would make out on my bed. I smiled when I saw the tear. I put the pillows back in their cases.

I walked over and closed the door. I wanted to unpack and put things away according to my own plan. I knew my mom would want to help, but I had to do this myself. I needed to know where things were. My clothes were the easy part---it was *everything else* that I wasn't sure of.

After I got my things sorted, I put on some comfy, nighttime threads: a worn-out tee I'd had forever and a pair of black and white checkered flannel bottoms.

I pulled myself together and went to join my family in the living room. They were anxious to talk to me. I was missing them terribly. It all balanced. I was so tired, but I knew I needed to give them some time.

"Rollie, those are some cool pants," my sister said. "Where'd you get them?"

"I got them at a store at the mall by school," I responded. "They've got all kinds of boss stuff. You'd be blown away!"

I sat down. My family unknowingly encircled me. I pushed back a little.

"What's wrong?" My mom asked.

"Nothing. I'm just..." I paused. "I'm OK."

My dad looked at me and asked, "Rollie, are you sure you're alright?"

"Yeah dad, I'm fine. I've just been a bit off lately," I said. "It's been tough... I don't know what to say. I'm sorry if I'm a little weird." I'd addressed my dad, but I was talking to everyone.

Devon gave me a look. "Rollo's just tired," she announced to the rest of my family.

Hearing her call me 'Rollo' freaked me out. The only person who'd ever called me that was Celia's mother. It was obvious that Devon had been with Celia recently---or so I wanted to believe.

"Yeah, Dev's right," I said. "I am tired. I'm sorry if I've ruined everyone's night." I sounded like a defeated man.

"Well, you should get some sleep, honey," my mom said. "You've had a long day. We've got plenty of time to catch up."

I nodded and stood up from my chair. I bid everyone goodnight and went to my bedroom. I shut the door and turned off the light. I got undressed and haphazardly left everything on the bed.

I rolled over onto my stomach and fell into Celia's pillow. I wept like I never had before. My tears poured into the pillow. As I cried into the cotton-covered, fluffy foam, I tried to draw Celia's scent from the fabric. I know my mother had washed these linens since I'd left, but my mind drifted back to the last time Celia was in this bed and how she'd left her smell all over the sheets and pillow. I pretended I could smell her as I wept. My God I missed her.

I was so confused about us. I was wondering if the word 'us' even applied to Celia and me anymore. I tried to draw a little more of her scent from deep within the fabric and filling. I fell asleep with that. It was all I had left for the moment.

CHAPTER 22

I woke up the next morning and everything seemed so quiet. I tried to get my focus and composure. Once I'd realized where I was, I sat up in bed. I was naked. I'd had a dream, but I don't remember it.

I could see through the window. It was white and out of focus. It looked like it snowed a bit last night---*my brother will be happy.*

I dropped back down and rolled over. I contemplated staying in bed longer. However, I eventually got up, got dressed and sat on the edge of the bed.

I was hungry. I think a lot of my hunger stemmed from my loss of a soul and dignity last night. I thought about the Danishes at the Sleepy Swan Inn the morning after grad night; the morning after---*after.*

I left my room. I smiled a legitimate smile as I took in the scent of eggs, bacon and pancakes---*breakfast!*

I walked into the kitchen and saw an enigmatic scene: a huge mess created by my mom and my sister. It was amazing, but so wrong. I couldn't help but chuckle.

"What are you laughing at?" My mom asked.

"You two," I said. "It's a scene I never thought I'd witness."

My mom smacked my arm. "Oh, you," she said. "A lot has changed since you've left."

I tested the boundaries. "Really?" I said. "So, if I left a mess around the house, you'd be OK with it?"

"No... well..." she paused. "Oh, why do you have to do this to me?"

I looked at her. "Some things will never ever change,

mom," I said. "No matter what."

"What do you want to have, Rollie?" Devon asked. "As you can see, we've got the *yoozh*."

"It all looks great," I said. "I'll have a couple of pancakes, an egg and a couple of slices of bacon to start. I'm pretty hungry."

"You want your egg hard fried?"

"Yeah. Just make sure it's super hard---no hint of yolky liquidity."

"I remember, dude. You haven't been gone that long."

Devon fried the egg and I sat and watched. I thought about offering to help, but the situation was fine without my interference.

While Devon fried my egg, she poured the batter for the pancakes. "Two, right?" She asked.

"Yep," I responded.

One pancake was perfectly round. The second one was misshapen. It had started out round but seemed to break from its intended form. There was a semi-circle at the top, while the center portion oozed into a curved, oval shape. I looked at it and it bothered me. I didn't know why.

"Sorry, dude, that other pancake looks weird," Devon said.

"It's OK," I said. "It'll eat the same."

Devon chuckled. "It kinda' looks P.G," she said.

I suddenly lost a bit of my appetite and let out an uneasy laugh.

"It does look a tad knocked-up," I said.

If I'd needed a point to initiate a conversation about Celia, this would be the best---and possibly worst---place to do it. I was surprised no one had mentioned her yet. Even last night her name never came up.

The front door opened. My mom and sister and I peered like three curious meerkats as my dad and brother walked in. They put their coats and boots in the alcove and were ready for breakfast.

Everyone was in and it was time to eat. We gathered our plates and sat at the table. No one talked initially. The only sounds were that of clinking silverware on porcelain, chewing and nose-breathing. I reached across the table for the syrup.

"Roland. I know you're struggling at school, but did you fail manners as well?" My mom asked coldly.

The vibe in the room changed with my faux pas.

"I'm sorry," I said. "Could you please pass the syrup?"

"Now, was that so hard?" My mom chirped.

"No. It was painless," I said, as I poured the syrup on my pancakes.

The mood in the room changed again. My mother went from being mayor of *Mannersville* and returned to kindly Mrs. McCallum.

"So, Roland, what would you like to do today? Any plans?" My mom asked, as she cut into her eggs. I watched the yolk bleed out of them and I cringed.

I felt that the way she'd asked me about my plans indicated I would be at my family's mercy: without a car and unable to do anything by myself. This was not going to happen.

"I was actually going to ask dad if I could have a car," I said. "I want to go into town."

My dad spoke, "I don't see why not. You can take the truck if you want."

Jerry chimed in, "I thought you wanted me to use the truck to haul wood today."

"I do, but Rollie can have it after that," my dad responded. "It shouldn't take more than an hour or two to get everything done."

"Thank you, dad," I said. "I have a couple of things I want to take care of. I want to go see David and Jeff, too. Surprise them. They don't know I'm home."

"Is there anything *special* you'd like to do while you're home?" My mom asked.

I felt like this was where I needed to address the *possible* elephant in the room.

"I want to see Celia," I said.

The mood changed again. The room went deathly quiet and everyone froze.

"What? You all had to know I'd want to see her," I said. "She's my girlfriend. I was surprised no one had mentioned her yet."

I looked around the table and saw the expressions on everyone's face. They were all different, and they were all disturbing.

My mom stared at my dad. It was as if she was trying to coax him into saying something. My dad looked lost. My sister looked upset. She looked as if she'd lost her best friend. My brother gave me that 'chicks, man,' look he'd tried before and failed with; however, this time it seemed to be working.

"Am I missing something?" I asked. "Besides Celia, that is."

My dad looked at me and said, "Rollie, I don't think it's a good idea for you to go over there."

My mom chimed in, "Honey, so much has changed since you left. So many things happened with Celia. It's best you just let it all go."

"Why?! She's my girlfr..." I paused. "No!" I exclaimed. "She's not my damn girlfriend, she's my *fiancée*. We're engaged! I haven't talked to---or heard from her in months. I miss her so much. I want to go see her!"

My mom covered her face. She talked into her hands, "Oh my God! Engaged?! You're not really engaged."

"We are mom. I asked her at the prom," I said. "I proposed to her for real the night we went out to the Sheraton. I gave her a diamond ring and everything."

"Why? When? When did you do all of this?" My mom asked. She shook her head in a panic.

"Why? Because I love her. You *know* that," I said. "As for when---I just told you---it was a few days after the prom. I stopped after work and bought the ring. I asked her when we went to dinner. It really happened."

My dad was upset, but not as pissed as he could've been. "So, that's why you were arguing with me at dinner on graduation night," he said.

"I didn't argue, dad. I just stated facts," I said. "I love her, and I've always known I wanted to be with her."

"No. No. This isn't happening," my mom said frantically.

"Mom, it's already happened," I stated. "It's happening as we speak."

"No, Roland. It. Is. Not. Happening," my mom said. The staccato in her voice was deliberate and matter of fact. I was sensing she was trying to tell me something beyond this conversation.

"Mom... what is it?" I asked. "This is about something else. Something more than just being upset about Celia and me being engaged."

My mom sat silently. I looked at my dad.

"Dad. What is going on?" I asked.

"Rollie. Celia is gone," he said solemnly.

"'Gone'? What does that mean?" I asked in shock.

"She's gone, son. She left home."

I looked at my mom. I couldn't believe what my dad was saying.

"Mom, is this true?" I asked.

My mom was tearing up. "Yes, honey, it is," she said. "But your father is being kind."

"What do you mean?" I asked.

"Celia didn't leave home," my mom said, looking down at the table. "She got thrown out."

"Thrown out?!" I asked frantically. "What the hell?! Her folks... why?!"

My parents were tight-lipped. I looked at my sister for help.

"Dev, what happened?" I asked. "You'd seen Celia since I'd left, right?"

"No. I talked to her a couple of times. We were supposed to get together and send you a care package. She never showed,"

Devon said. She began to cry. "We saw her at the store, but she didn't see us. She was..."

My mom quickly shushed her. It seemed odd.

"So why would her parents throw her out?" I asked.

Silence again.

"What did she do?" I asked. "What could she have done that would make her parents throw her out into the street?"

Silence.

"For the love of God---somebody tell me something!" I yelled, as I smacked my hands on the table. "That's it. I'm so done with this. I'm going to see her folks and find out what the hell is going on."

My mom yelled, "STOP! ROLAND, STOP!"

"DAMMIT! PLEASE TELL ME WHAT'S GOING ON!" I shouted. Devon covered her ears and cried for me to stop. My dad grabbed my arm. He pulled me back into my chair and told me to settle down.

"She got pregnant, Roland. Celia got pregnant after you left, and her parents threw her out. *That's* what happened," my mom said sounding eerily calm. "She went and found another guy and got pregnant after you left."

I knew now why my mother was so quick to silence Devon. I closed my eyes and took a deep breath. My parents didn't want to hear that Celia and I were engaged. They would certainly not want to hear what I had to say next.

"I know Celia was pregnant," I said. "She didn't get pregnant after I left. Celia was pregnant with *my* baby."

I thought my mom was going to faint. My dad shook his head in confusion. My brother sat lost and looked like he wished he was somewhere else. My sister smiled through her tears. I heard her whisper: "I'm gonna' be an aunt!"

The atmosphere became abruptly somber. It felt like a post-battle scene in a movie. Grainy, coated with an imaginary haze and thick with a monotonous, ambient ring.

"Does anybody know where she went?" I asked.

"No. She left town and no one has seen her since," my dad

said. He was still holding my arm.

"I'm gonna' go kick the shit out of her dad---that cock-sucker," I said. I could feel my eyes fill with blood. The somber mood of the room destroyed.

My mom flushed with shock at my words.

"Oh, my God mom... I'm so sorry," I said.

I jumped from my chair. I went around the table to hug my mother. "I'm so angry right now," I said, as my eyes welled with tears. "I'm sorry you had to hear that. I'm so, so sorry."

As I hugged my mom, she cried on me as well.

My dad got up from the table and left the room. He was gone for a minute or two. When he returned, he put his hand on my shoulder and patted me.

"Rollie, I have something for you," he said quietly.

My dad grabbed me and pulled me away from the table.

"This came in the mail a few weeks ago," he said. "Does that handwriting look familiar?"

I studied the envelope. It was powder blue and very thick. There was no return address. The stamp was placed up-side-down. It was cancelled with a Connecticut postmark. It all looked so foreign. However, I did indeed recognize the hand-writing.

"Why didn't anyone tell me about this?" I asked. "Why didn't you forward it to me at school?"

"We didn't know what to make of it," my dad said. "Devon recognized Celia's writing, but we thought it best to wait to give you the letter."

"Why? Didn't you think it was important to me?"

"We didn't know how... how deep you two were in."

"Christ, dad. 'How deep?' We're not double agents. We were just in love. She and I planned our lives together while everyone told us to sow our oats apart."

My dad breathed deep. "Maybe you should read the letter, Rollie," he said. "It might give you the answers you're looking for."

I nodded. "I'll do that," I said. "Can I have some time

alone, please?"

My mom suggested I go read the letter in my room. I didn't think that was a good idea. I wanted to be *alone,* but I wanted my family around should the words I was reading prove too much to take.

I placed the letter on the counter and returned to the table. I wanted to finish my breakfast. My family was surprised. I told them I needed a moment to prepare. I needed to build up my strength. I was a hungry college student. Decent, home cooked meals were a blessing. I wasn't going to let this delicious food go to waste---even for a letter from Celia. Truth be told: the letter was already written. It had been here for a few weeks. My finishing breakfast was not going to change what Celia had said. It was not going to make her words any easier to take.

I cleaned my plate. I offered to help my mom and sister clear the table and do the dishes. My mom declined my help. I asked again. I was cavalier about the letter earlier, but now I feared it. I wanted to delay reading it for as long as I could.

My mom was upset with me. She couldn't believe I would be so careless. She wouldn't admit how she felt, but I knew it. My dad sat in his chair. I knew he was angry with me as well. Both of my parents were livid with me because of what they deemed as indiscretions and irresponsible behavior. It wasn't like that, though. However, no matter what I'd told them, they wouldn't believe me. Carelessness and being foolish was not the reason for what had happened.

Celia getting pregnant was a happy accident that turned sour. She never told me the truth about our baby. When I'd brought it up, she cut me off. If only she'd been honest, I would've dropped out of school and eloped with her. I would've gotten a job or joined the military. I would've made sure we had what we needed to make a good life for us and our little one. She knew how much I loved her.

I never understood why she felt she couldn't tell me any-thing. I didn't... *I just didn't.* Maybe she did. Maybe she chose to keep things from me so that I would not make any undue sacrifices? Why would she do that? I didn't care about anything but her. Maybe she thought that if I'd quit school or given up something for her that I would resent her. I would be miserable. I would hate her and our child. *No, my love, I hate my life* without *you and our child.* I hated school already.

My family dispersed. Even though they were all in the house, I was essentially alone. I stared at the envelope. I know Celia wrote the letter, but the impersonal lack of a return address gave me second thoughts. The upside-down stamp---the unspoken postal symbol for 'I love you,' brought me back around.

I sat still in my chair but was being thrown in every direction. I picked up the envelope and followed the lines and curves of Celia's handwriting. I'd reached the last number of my folks' zip code and I felt a chill run down my spine. I finally opened the envelope.

I pulled out the letter. The yellow legal papers burst, getting bigger as I removed them. There was a lot more than the envelope let on. At first, I breathed deep. I was hoping to draw the scent of Celia's perfume from the letter. This was not to happen. She did not spray her sweet, bottled pheromones on these papers. It made me sad. I unfolded the pages but was not ready to read them. I needed something to numb me. I knew what she'd written was not something I'd wanted to read.

I wished Brett was here---he'd have some booze. My parents had booze. That was what I needed before I could read Celia's words. I opened the liquor cabinet and grabbed a bottle of scotch. I cracked the cap and took a swig. It burned, but it wouldn't burn as much as I knew Celia's words would. My eyes teared up. I pulled the bottle from the cabinet and poured myself a glass. I swirled the glass and took a sip. I was ready. I was ready to read the words that Celia couldn't say to me.

CHAPTER 23

My love… my dearest, Roland Jacob,

Please forgive me for not writing or calling you sooner. I also want to apologize for all the stupid letters that I did write. You deserved better than what I sent you. Please forgive me for what I'm about to tell you. Please forgive me for EVERYTHING. It's taken me so long to write this letter. I didn't know what to say, or where to start. So, I'll start at the beginning---or the end, depending on how you want to look at it. Back to the night you left and why I didn't come to the airport.

I was afraid. I was afraid that if we saw each other you'd change your mind about leaving. I wanted that, but then again, I didn't. You were going away and you were doing it for us. I know that <u>now</u> but didn't want to accept it then. I couldn't bear to see you one last time, only to have to watch you go. It was just easier to stay home. I cried so much after you left. Remember your t-shirt you let me wear that one time? Well, I kept it and I wore it and I cried into it for days after you left. I could still smell you in the fabric, even though I'd washed it a couple of times. Does that make sense? It sounds stupid. I'm sorry. Patty told me how I would regret not seeing you. She said I was being selfish. She was right---about everything. Speaking of selfish, I played with myself a few times after you left. I even used your shirt once!!! It felt nice to have an orgasm, but it wasn't like when you did it to me. I guess I am a full-fledged slut, now! HA! Sorry. Anyway, that's why I didn't come to see you. I wanted to. I just couldn't.

Speaking of school, I hope it is going OK. I know you didn't want to go, but I also know it was to make yourself better---a better artist and person. You didn't need any help, but <u>the world</u> said you *did. I understand it better now. I hope you do, too.*

So many things have happened since you left. I don't know where to begin, because nothing was all that great. I spent time at home a lot. I argued with my parents about everything. My momma noticed my ring. She got mad and slapped me. She told me I was stupid and needed to stop dreaming. She said you were too much of a dreamer and your bad influences were rubbing off on me. Momma apologized, but we weren't OK after that---you can probably understand. Daddy wasn't mad, though. See, I told you he liked you. He just wondered if you were going to ask him for my hand. I told him you'd tried, but the timing was never right. I figured you'd do it when you came home for break. You don't have to now.

So, what I guess I'm saying is that my folks know we got engaged. They were sorta' upset at first---one more than the other---but they got over it. Did you ever tell your family? What did they say? I'll bet Devon was happy. I really love your little sister; she's like my best friend. You probably didn't say anything, though. I know you too well. You would want to wait until the time was right, like to ask my daddy. We're so different like that. I wanted to tell everyone about us. You made me so happy. I wanted the world to know. I love you!!!

I stopped reading and took another drink of the scotch. I was confused by what Celia had written. It made sense but seemed so difficult and cryptic---like the last letters she'd written me at school. I picked up the page and flipped it over. The following paragraphs were written in blue ink. Celia had obviously changed pens. I didn't know if she'd taken a break, or her pen had run out of ink. Knowing her, she'd stopped, came back and misplaced her pen. This made me smile. I could see her searching for this pen she'd just set down. *It was right there.* She'd probably seen it twice in her search. I could picture her crinkling her nose in frustration, huffing and grabbing another pen. That was my Celia.

Momma wanted to throw a party for us---can you believe that? She freaked out on me; then wanted to have a social for us to announce our engagement. It was crazy. My momma is crazy---but you know that. I told her no, maybe later. We needed to figure things out before we went and did something like that. Now that I think about it, maybe I wasn't ready to tell the world. Not to sound like that, my love. I really DID want everyone to know, but maybe it was best to wait. I don't know. I don't know anything. I just remember the night at dinner when you proposed. It was so romantic.

I think about you every day, do you know that? I really miss you and you're always on my mind. I would sing that song to myself sometimes when I thought of you. I know how much you hate Willie Nelson---so I'd pretend it was Elvis for you! HA! I always wonder what you're up to. I try to picture you working on things at school. Pens and paints everywhere. I think about what you're doing, and it reminds me of Darren from Bewitched. *He was an advertiser, too. I don't think he did the artwork, though. I'm trying to do that nose thing Samantha does---I can't. If I could I'd do it. I'd make you appear here, right in my bedroom! We could make love again! I'd make everyone disappear so we would be alone. I miss making love with you. Do you miss it, too? Of course, you do! You're a guy and guys like to do it all the time! HA! I have to go. I'll write more tomorrow...*

Her writing stopped midway through the page. It seemed dramatic. The day itself had become the paper. I set the letter down for a moment. I still had no idea what I was reading.

Celia sounded calm, albeit a bit scatterbrained, but that was her sometimes. At this point, it was completely understandable.

My mom came into the kitchen to check on me.

"Roland, are you OK?" She asked. She spied my glass of scotch and commented, "liquid courage?"

"Yeah, unfortunately. It seems to be one of the things I did manage to learn at school," I said, tapping on the glass. "As for me being 'OK,' I'm not sure. I don't know what I'm reading."

"What has she said so far, if you don't mind me asking?"

"Nothing, mom. Nothing really tangible. It just sounds like a choppy love letter."

"Well, is that bad?"

"It is if you're looking for answers. Other than that, it's fine."

"Which do you want? Answers, or to feel fine?"

"I want both. I want to know what happened. I want to know we still have a future."

My mom scowled a little. "Honey, you're in trouble. *She's* in trouble. Your futures are in a major flux at the moment," she said. "You're failing in school; Celia's pregnant and obviously not even in this state anymore; you're here with a lot of questions; *we* have a lot of questions for you. I don't think any outcome is going to be good."

"What does that mean, mom? There has to be something positive here. There has to be something I can do to make this right," I stated. "Celia and I love each other. And whether anyone likes it or not, she's pregnant with my child."

"Roland," my mom said, closing her eyes. "I know you want a happy ending but consider the facts---it just isn't going to happen, son. Not the way you're hoping for. I'm so sorry to have to say that."

"So far what she's said has been OK," I said, defending Celia and her words.

"'So far.' But you've only gotten through one page of that letter and there's a lot more to read," my mom said. She put her head on my shoulder. "There are some things a mother's love cannot fix and this is one of them. I'll be here when you're finished with Celia's letter and that booze. Unfortunately, the pain will be, too. We'll work through it."

My mom left the room and I returned to the letter. I was not going to buy into what my mother was selling. There had to be something good to come from this. I knew things were amiss, but I also knew that this was Celia and me: we could get through this no matter what.

Hi! I apologize for that. I was supposed to write you the next day, but things have been crazy. I had to go and do a few things. I lost track of time. So, it's been like three days since I stopped writing. Where was I? Oh yeah, sex. I mentioned sex. You made me like it, Roland! OK, I have to stop. I'm getting worked up!!! No. Wait! I want to talk about it. I mentioned I missed making love with you. I think a lot about the first time we spent the night together at the Sleepy Swan and it brings back so many wonderful memories. You made me feel like a princess---I think I told you that? Did I? Well, you did! It hurt a lot---but it felt so good. When you made love to me, I became a different person. Not like that! But like, you made me feel free and loved--- it's like something magical. It was like being on the swings as an adult---that kind of feeling. I pretended I was your love slave and you could have your way with me---I was your virgin sacrifice! No one else can ever say that, you know! You have something of mine that no other man can ever have. I'm so glad you were my first, Roland. Do you know that? I'm glad it was you---really you.

After we did it the first time, I wanted more. I wanted to feel you inside me all the time. There were so many other things to do! I know I got kinda' weird afterwards---not calling and everything. I just wasn't sure what to do. I loved it so much and that scared me. I didn't want you to think I'd become hussy... well, if I did, I'd be your hussy! HA! The last time we did it was amazing, too! I still can't believe I did THAT to you! You know what THAT I'm talking about, too---I'm not going to say it! If you could see me now---I'm totally blushing. I wonder how you're feeling. Are you feeling like I do now? If you want to go and masturbate, you can. Think of me when you do it---if you do it. It's OK. I want you to think of me every time you come. Maybe I could masturbate too and touch this paper with my fingers? It would smell like my pussy---I can't believe I just said that word! Geez! I sound like my sister! I better not do that---it might get nasty when it dries. I'll do it, but not touch the paper. I need a moment, my love.

I had to believe that Celia actually took a break from writing to get herself off. I had gotten an erection as I read, and I did want to masturbate. However, what I did was take a breath and another drink. What I really needed was a cold shower.

The more of Celia's letter I read, the better I was feeling. I felt instilled with hope and confidence as the pages advanced. She'd asked for my forgiveness at the beginning. Now I wasn't sure why she was asking for it. I sensed her redemption with each passing paragraph. I finally understood why she stayed away after we'd made love the first time. Everything that had been clouded was now becoming clear. I found my spot and read the last couple sentences on the page.

Hee hee! I did it! You don't know if I'm lying or not, but I'm going to plant the image in your head anyway---you get to watch me touch myself in your dreams! You like that, I know!

I've got a doctor's appointment tomorrow. I'm OK---just want to make sure everything is fine. It's a 'lady appointment,' so I won't bore you with all the girl stuff. I should probably stop here for the day. I put one thing in your head, then wreck it with medical stuff. Sorry! Just forget I mentioned the doctor, OK?! I'll write more tomorrow, Roland. I promise. Goodnight my love!

Unlike the last 'day break' in the pages, Celia continued writing on the page I was reading. She'd drawn a wavy line and hearts to split the text.

Well, it really is tomorrow! I haven't dated this, so I could be lying again, but I'm not. It really is the next day. My appointment went well and I'm totally healthy and everything is where it's supposed to be, so that's all that matters. I've put on some weight, though. I'm a little bigger than I was before you left. My momma always said I was too skinny anyway. What do you think? I don't have a picture to show you how different I look. It's not bad---I'm just meatier than I was before. More of me to love, I guess?!

Speaking of getting fat, how are you eating at school? I know how you can be. Are you getting enough food? I'll bet your eating crazy college food like chips and popcorn all the time---and pizza, too! When you have pizza, do you think about me? I miss our Tuesdays: pizza and milkshakes. Guess I don't need the milkshakes anymore! You know why! HA! My friends and I went out for pizza a few times since I've moved here, but it's not the same. Nothing has been since I left home.

I flipped the page over, and Celia had changed to black ink again. I hadn't read her words yet, but I looked over the paper. It was smudged and blotted. There were several places on the page where the side of Celia's palm had caught ink, leaving patchy prints. Her penmanship was no longer what it had been. It now seemed desperate and hastened. The letter had gone from a somewhat fluid state, to one I didn't recognize. I felt a twinge in my chest. Perhaps this was *truly the letter*---the letter my mother tried to prepare me for. I refused to believe it. However, the only way I'd be able to know and prove my mother wrong about Celia was to read it.

I've had a terrible day. It's been a couple of days since I wrote, and I've been sick about everything. I haven't been honest with you Roland. I haven't been lying to you---I just haven't told you everything that's been going on. I wanted so much to write you a happy letter. The letter I never wrote to you at school, the one you deserved. For as much as you deserved the happy letter, you deserve the truth even more. I told you nothing's been the same since I left home, and that's been true. All the other things I told you about: wanting to make love to you, how I miss you, that I love you---that's all true too! It really is!!! I swear to God!!! But no matter what I say to you, or how I tell how I still feel for you, it won't change the fact that I'm no good anymore. I'm not. I'm so... <u>Please don't stop reading. I beg you.</u> You can hate me all you want after you finish this, but please---PLEASE--- listen to what I have to say, OK?! <u>Promise me!</u> My love, please say you'll promise! I know you will because you always keep your prom- ises---not like me.

"I promise..." I said quietly.

After you left for school everything was OK for a few days. I started getting sick, though and I knew why. I was having <u>morning sickness</u>. That's right! I was pregnant! I got---<u>no, WE</u>---got pregnant the night we made love in your car. I can say 'we.' I know only mar-

ried couples say 'we,' but we were close enough. It really happened! I was so happy! I wanted your baby inside me. I wanted to have something of you to carry with me while you were gone. You wanted that too, I know. You needed it, too---so we'd have that connection! I know you believe that! My sister asked me why I was sick a lot. Momma knew almost immediately. No matter what I did to hide things, she knew. She's had four kids. She's a country broad---she knows this stuff. I tried to deny it and just said I had the flu.

Sarah took me to the doctor and my test results were positive. I was so excited but so scared. I told Sarah it was your baby. <u>She's the only one who knew the truth.</u> My love, what I'm going to tell you next is very bad---but I had to do it. <u>I had to!!!</u> Please forgive me!!!

I stopped reading again. I started crying. I took a long drink from my glass. I drained it. I poured some more scotch, filling the glass halfway. My eyes would go no further down the page. It was as if a barricade had dropped between the last sentence I'd read and the one that came next.

What could she have done?! What did she do to our baby?! There was no way Celia got an abortion. I'd played this scenario in my head before. Her family would scorn her and treat her like shit for getting pregnant, but they were too rooted in values, traditions and the church to allow her to commit such a sin.

If she'd miscarried, that was not her fault---that was God's. I didn't believe in God like Celia did, but I wanted to believe that He would never do something so cruel to us. I took another drink and continued reading.

It was only a matter of time before everyone knew I was really pregnant. I couldn't get you caught up in everything. I couldn't let you destroy yourself at school worrying about me and the baby. That wasn't fair to you...

My head shook in disbelief and I threw the page I was reading onto the floor.

"WASN'T FAIR TO ME?!" I yelled. "YOU NOT TELLING ME

ABOUT OUR BABY WASN'T FAIR TO ME, CELIA!"

I heard a door open and my sister's voice.

"Are you OK?" Devon asked timidly.

"No," I said. "And I don't think I ever will be."

I heard Devon shut her door. There was silence once again. I picked up the page and continued reading.

...You had so much to worry about. I know this was for us--- it was all for us, but I wanted you to get through your first semester of school before I said anything. I wasn't sure what I would do, but I knew I could make it work. I wanted to come to you, but I couldn't--- I couldn't do that to you. It was so difficult, though. It was getting to where I had to do something. I had to fix things. I had to---please understand, Roland, please! I had to make things right for you and me and the baby.

I CHEATED ON YOU! I WAS UNFAITHFUL!!! Before I could let things become too 'obvious,' I went out with a guy my daddy knew from work. He's an architect---he's a kind of an artist. I guess I have a thing for artists? He's got a good job. I met him one day when I went to see daddy at work. He introduced us and I was not interested. I'm still not!!! But I knew I had to do something to make a big problem just a little smaller. We went out and I seduced him. We slept together on our first date and... And I told everyone that's who got me pregnant. He doesn't even know he's not the baby's father.

"You fucking whore," I mumbled. I wanted to stop reading this letter altogether, but I had to know more. I didn't even fathom that Celia would sleep with another man, let alone do it while we were still together. The letter had gone from a somewhat pleasant drive to a multi-car pile-up. It couldn't possibly get any worse.

After I told my parents that I was pregnant and it was the guy daddy worked with, everything went crazy at home. My momma called me terrible things and blamed YOU at first. She said that you had done this to me. She said she didn't believe me that the baby was this other guy's and that it was yours. I lied to protect you. I lied to make momma and daddy not think of you like that. But I wanted them to know it WAS yours!!! I wanted them to know we made love and we were going to have a family!!! We were going to get married!!! And more than anything---I loved YOU!!! I didn't want this guy---I hated pretending! I still hate it! I just kept on saying the baby was his until I'd convinced everyone---even myself of it. I feel so terrible and sick about it. I hated what I'd done.

I shoved the page onto the floor and angrily picked up page three. I could stop any time. I'd gotten my answers. I'd just called Celia a *fucking whore*. I despised myself for what I'd said. There was more, however. She had written more pages and I had to know what those pages said. By now, it was painfully obvious that my mom was right: I was not going to get my happy ending, but I had to know just how far from it I'd land once I was done falling to earth.

It's been a couple of days. I needed a break and I think you did too. I'm so very sorry Roland. I know you must hate me. I can't blame you. Please let me finish telling you what happened, OK?
Well, my parents and I fought all the time and they decided it was best if I left. My momma said: 'let the guy who knocked you up take care of you.' My mother said this to me! My mother, who was not the purest lamb in the flock---she said this. Did you know she got pregnant young, too? It's true---twice! And she judges me?! Big Kenny is not my real dad. He's not Patty's dad either. Did you know that? He adopted us later, right after K.J. was born. I felt so slighted. My momma should've understood. She didn't. She always said you reminded her of my real daddy---I think that's why she was so awful to you---and why she's still being awful to you. I never knew him, but I know that my real daddy would've never done the things that Mr. Kenneth Chandler did to me and Patty when we were little.

My jaw dropped. I stopped reading. Did I want to go any further? Did I really want to know what this man---a man I'd stood up for and defended on numerous occasions---had done to his 'daughters'? My rage towards her parents had escalated while I'd read this letter. Now it had gone high-yield and I was harboring very violent tendencies. The letter had gone from the aforementioned pleasant drive, subsequent multi-car pile-up, and now there appeared to be the possibility of fatalities.

He did horrible things to me and Patty. I don't want to tell you, because I think you already know. He did it a lot. My momma didn't know anything for a long time until she caught him. She was pregnant with my brother. Momma threatened to kill Big Kenny. He left us alone after that, but we didn't forget. I know I <u>couldn't</u> forget. After K.J. was born, Big Kenny adopted Patty and me. My momma said that made us 'his kids,' officially. He couldn't touch us anymore. He couldn't molest us if we were his daughters. We all believed it, because he stopped. I think I know why he liked you so much---he was afraid of you. He knew how much you loved me and would kill him if you knew what he'd done. He respected you, too. He knew you were good for me and wanted to make me happy. He saw you as my way out from him.

Tears spilled from my eyes and onto the paper. They hit the yellow, inked pulp like raindrops. I did not brush them away. I didn't want to smear the ink. My emotions were so fragmented right now. I didn't know what I was feeling. Reading Celia's letter was like riding a blind rollercoaster. Every hill and curve was obscured until you hit it, and they were all sharp and jarring.

"Jesus. That explains why he was always giving me accolades," I whispered. "He *really did* want me to rescue Celia from him. I just didn't know how in need of rescue she was. I'm so sorry, my love. I should've killed him that day I..."

Well none of that mattered now. I was the bad one. My parents allied against me. They told me they didn't want me to 'be like that,' so they threw me out. I moved in with Sarah for a couple of weeks, but I'd also been seeing the guy, too. He asked me to move in him. I said yes. Roland, I'm so sorry. I just got myself in so deep. I didn't know what to do.

We got married in September. You were a few weeks into school when it happened. I was still getting your letters at home. Patty took care of them and hid them so I could write you back. And calling? I couldn't. I could never talk. There was always someone around. That's why I was so weird when you called me and we did talk.

When Patty played your tape for me, I cried so hard. You sounded so wonderful. Hearing your voice made me so happy. I kept answering your questions to me. I felt like we were talking. I loved the songs. I copied the music so I could have a tape of it. K.J was impressed. He was surprised that I'd be listening to some of the songs. I almost slipped and told him you sent me the tape. Deep down, I think he knew you did. I don't know.

You know I still love you. I still love you so much. When I feel the baby inside me, I know it's you and that keeps me happy. My husband is OK. He's nice and takes good care of me, but he's <u>not</u> you. <u>He never will be</u>. I want you to know that when I have sex with him it's <u>meaningless</u>. We don't do it very often, but I do get pregnant woman 'urges,' and well... It is part of my job as a wife, even though I don't love him---or it. I'll never tell you that I think about you when we're in bed. I don't. I can't. I think about you when I'm alone and touch myself. I pretend it's you making me come. There's no way he could ever do that to me.

I was so livid. I was beside myself with what I'd just read, but a tiny part of me felt warm. I felt like I truly was Celia's first and last and always. There were new and appalling things I'd learned, but I couldn't help but push my anger aside for a moment and focus on the fact that she *still loved me.* She was pregnant with my baby. She would always think of me. For as devastated, angry and homicidal as I was at the moment; I had a happy fragment to keep me from doing anything *too* irrational. I placed the fragment with the fiber of hope I'd culled last night.

I looked over the next few pages and there was no text. Celia just drew a bunch of cute pictures of little faces, hearts, flowers and clouds. She wrote our names in fancy script. She wrote *Celia Loves Roland Forever* in a heart. She made a lattice design that when you turned the paper it spelled *True Love*.

She placed a paper placemat in amongst the pages as well. It was from one of the places we went for pizza. She wrote little notes on it and circled her favorite toppings. I began to cry again.

There were several pages of drawings and doodles to look at. I went through them all. They were wonderful---and absolutely meaningless. When I reached the last page of the letter, Celia returned to writing.

Did you like my drawings? I'll never be as good as you! I want to say thank you for reading this. If you got to this last page, I'm so happy. I told you things I'd kept hidden---things you had to know--- for better or worse. Roland, I know I keep asking you to, but PLEASE FORGIVE ME for everything I've done---especially all of the things I've done to hurt you. You deserve better than what I've done. Maybe momma was right: I am the bad one.

I apologize for sending this letter to your parents' house, but I didn't have your address at school anymore. I cannot tell you where I am right now. My husband and I have moved. I can't tell you his name or anything like that, because I don't want you to come and try to find me, OK. I love you Roland Jacob McCallum with all my heart and soul. I will have your baby soon and even though you'll never see it, always know that it is yours and will be the most enduring part of my life.

Before I forget to say it---I want to thank you Roland, my love. You may not realize it, but you made me find the person I wanted to be. The person I never thought I could be until I met and fell in love with you. You made me strong---you made me a woman. I know that sounds old-fashioned and cliché, but it's true. Even though things in my life recently have turned out the way they did, without the strength you brought out of me---I wouldn't have survived any of it. I'd like to say I'm happy, but that would be a lie and you would know it was a lie. I will be happy someday and so will you. I just know it.

I'm sad to say that this will be the last you'll hear from me. It has to be this way. Please understand, my love. I know it's hard, but I know you do.

I will always, always, ALWAYS love you!!! (If you ever hear Dolly Parton sing that song, please think of me!) Don't ever forget that, promise me. Whenever you have pizza, pull off a little bit to remind you of me. Have a milkshake, too! Think of me forever. I will think of you twice as much.

Always and Forever---Your Love.
Celia Beth.

CHAPTER 24

I gathered the papers, folded them up tightly and put them back into the envelope. I slipped the flap into the back and set my hands atop of it. The address and stamp were facing the counter. I did not want to see Celia's handwriting, nor did I want to see the upside-down stamp. I did not want to be reminded of the symbolism. I did not want to be reminded of Celia at the moment. I'd read her last words to me. I didn't want to see the ones that brought this letter here.

I finished my scotch. I was so upset and disconnected, I didn't feel the burn of the liquor as it channeled down my throat and into my gut. I sat. I looked around and saw that I was still alone. I sighed and dropped my head onto Celia's letter. I began to sob. I tried not to get tears on this letter, but it was impossible. I felt a hand on my shoulder and heard the words: "Dude... it's gonna' be OK."

I turned in my chair and fell into my sister's arms. She held me tight as I cried on her. I shook and kept asking "why?" She didn't say anything. She knew what was going on. She knew better than anyone.

"Dev... she's gone... gone," I cried. "She's married... *she's married*... what did I do wrong?"

"You didn't do anything," Devon said. "Stuff was going on... I don't know."

"I'm going to kill her folks. You know what her dad did to her?" I asked.

"I... don't know... I just know some bad stuff was happening."

"I'm going over to the Chandlers'. I need to..."

"Rollie, you can't. You just can't."

"Why, Dev? I'm not going to do anything stupid. I promise."

"You can't go over to their house. Please, just trust me on this."

"Tell me why, Dev. Come on, be straight with me. You're the only one I can get a straight answer from, don't do this to me."

Devon was quiet. She closed her eyes tight and took a breath.

"It's just no good," she said.

I was frustrated beyond reason. Everybody knows everything except for me. I want answers. Nobody is talking.

My mom and dad came into the room and joined Devon. They too, reasoned mysteriously about why I shouldn't go to the Chandler's house.

"Rollie, nothing good will come of this if you go over there," my dad said. "There's nothing left. It's over."

"No, dad. I can't let this go. What Celia said in her letter..." I paused. "I need to know... I need something." I was rambling.

"Listen to you father and your sister. Better still: listen to what Celia said in her letter, honey," my mom said. "Please don't do this. You'll regret it---you'll regret it for the rest of your life."

My dad relented---to a point. "Son, if you really have to do this---do it tomorrow, OK? You drank half of a bottle of scotch; you're angry and heartbroken," he said. "This is not a good time. There's no way you're driving and you're not being rational."

I conceded. I was angry and beyond heartbroken---and quite tipsy. I thought about asking Jerry to take me to Celia's, but I put it to rest---at least for today.

"OK, OK. You all are right. I'll go tomorrow. You can't stop me from going, OK. You can't," I said unequivocally. "I'm going to confront her parents. I need to know what went on after I left."

"You may not get what you want, Roland," my mom said.

"Don't be upset if you turn up empty."

"I'm still going to try," I said sternly. "I want to know how Celia's parents could've done what they did. I have to find out. I have to face her dad. He did things he has to answer for."

Whatever my folks and my sister were trying to tell me, I wasn't listening. Nothing they said registered. I heard their words, but they may have well been speaking Russian to me: a different language; a different alphabet. My head hurt. It was a combination of this scuffle with my family, Celia's letter and the booze. I needed to lie down. I'd only been awake for a few hours, but I needed to get some sleep.

I went to my room and fell onto my bed. I stared at the ceiling like I was staring to Heaven. In my head I tried to conjure images of Celia, but they were scant and hard to focus. I wanted to imagine her in profile. I wanted to see her belly: full and wide with my baby growing inside her. I couldn't do it. I couldn't get my brain to produce what I wanted to see. I began to think of Celia in bed with someone else. These thoughts were fuzzy as well, but I could see her face. She was blank and distant while this other person lay atop of her, amateurishly trying to fuck her, but failing. He kept falling out of her. He was missing the mark entirely. She said she'd never think of me when she had sex with her husband---now I knew why.

"Get off of her," I whispered angrily. "Get your filthy body off of my Celia."

I couldn't go to sleep now. These visions I'd planted in my head would only get worse if I slept. I continued staring at the ceiling. However, my buzz was stronger than I thought. Soon, I could feel myself get light and eventually, I did fall asleep.

CHAPTER 25

I woke up with a jolt. I did not dream and that was a good thing. I was still upset over Celia's letter: what she'd said and done; the things she told me about her family. I put my head into my hands and started to cry again. I'd cried more today than I can remember. I looked at the clock. I'd slept for a couple of hours.

I left my room and no one was around. I put on my coat and boots and went outside. It looked like it had snowed a little more since this morning. There was not a lot, but enough to crunch beneath my feet. The sun was out, and I raised my face to it. The warm rays felt like a soft, wet caress on my face. It felt like Celia's touch when we first dated. This brought more tears to my eyes, but it also made me smile.

I walked around the yard a little. Everything looked different. When I left, it was still summer. It was hot and humid. The trees were full with leaves and the grass was lush and needed a mow. Now it was winter. It was cold and dry, but mild. The trees were bare; the sky was a patchwork of steel blue, stark white and thick, ash gray. Snow covered the gold, dormant grass. I'd lived through several winters at this house, but this one was different. It may be unseasonably warm for everyone else this year, but for me this was becoming the coldest winter I'd ever experienced.

My brother pulled up in my dad's truck. He had wood for the fireplace in the bed.

"Rollie! Hey man, I need a hand with this stuff," Jerry said, as he got out of the cab.

"I don't want to get my hands dirty," I said peering at the

wood.

"Come on! Here..." Jerry said, as he threw me a pair of worker's gloves. "Now your little girly palms will stay *holdibly soft*, or whatever that commercial says."

I rubbed my hands together and put the gloves on.

"You know I was going to help anyway," I said.

"I never know if your joking or not anymore," Jerry retorted.

"There's a lot of that going around."

"I'm glad your home little brother. I just wished your circumstances were better."

"Me too, Jerr."

"I didn't know there was *so much* going on. No offense, but I've been trying to steer clear of it all. It's not my place. It's a lot to take."

"No offense taken. It *is* a lot. At least it's all out there, now. Everyone knows the truth."

Jerry and I stopped talking and went back to work. We kept working silently for a few minutes. I marveled at all the firewood as I grabbed the small, cut logs and pulled them from the truck bed. I hadn't done this for a while. I never remembered Jerry doing it at all.

It was nice to be outside helping my brother. I missed him. I missed being home. This little bit of manual labor was enhanced by the brisk December breeze which began to swell as we unloaded the truck. I wondered where all the wood came from.

"Dad chop all of this?" I asked.

"No, we got a guy now," Jerry said. "Dad hates chopping wood."

"Can't say I blame him. Do you remember me telling you about...?" I stopped mid-sentence.

"Remember telling me about what?" Jerry inquired.

"Nothing..." I said somberly.

What I couldn't share with Jerry was a memory I'd had about helping Celia's dad split logs. Big Kenny had a bunch of wood to split and asked me to help him. I'd never done it before and thought it would be cool. It was alright. Big Kenny got wasted and I ended up splitting most of the logs.

Celia's mother seemed impressed that I could figure out how to do the task 'all by my lonesome.' It wasn't difficult: stand log, split log, repeat. *Golly, even a soft-handed, ol' romantic artiste like me can foller them directions, ma'am.*

Celia, however, was *genuinely* impressed. She looked at me in awe; like I was a stud lumberjack who'd just chopped down half a forest---a hard-workin' man. To reward my labor, she fixed me a wonderful dinner, complete with strawberry shortcakes for dessert.

The smell of this wood was making me sick. I wonder if Big Kenny still has that splitter? If he does, I may just use it on his and Tina's heads tomorrow.

"You OK?" Jerry asked. "I lost you for a second."

"I'm OK. Let's just get this stuff taken care of," I said, as I grabbed another log from the truck and threw it to the ground.

Jerry noticed the change in my demeanor. He said he'd wanted to 'steer clear' of my situation, but he couldn't.

"Rollie, if you need to talk to someone not named 'mom' or 'dad,' I'm right here," Jerry said. "You know you can count on me to listen. I hate seeing you like this."

"Thanks, man. I'm good," I said. "Besides, I wouldn't even know where to start with all of it."

"I know you read Celia's letter. What did it say?"

"Jerr, it said more than I could've hoped for and everything I'd wanted to hear."

"Well, that's good, right?"

"Yeah, to a point. Then she went into some other shit and it just..." I paused.

"It's OK," Jerry said. "You don't have to say anything else."

"Can you believe I'm going to be a father?"

Jerry shook his head. "No. That blew me away," he said.

"Me, too---a little," I responded.

"Did you know? You had to have known something."

"Yeah, I knew. Celia just never talked about it."

"I don't want to sound like a dick, but are you sure it's yours?"

"I had unprotected sex with her before I left. I *know* it's mine. Besides that, she told me."

"What are you going to do?"

"Nothing. She's married. She took care of that for me," I said, with a deep sigh.

"Oh my God, Rollie." Jerry said. He walked over and gave me a hug. "That freakin' sucks... all around... it absolutely, freakin' sucks."

I began to cry again. "More than you can possibly imagine," I said.

I sat by the fire and warmed myself while my family watched TV. My sister joined me. She brought me a glass of egg nog and sat by my side.

"Thought you might like this," Devon said. "Mom said I couldn't put any booze in it for you."

"It's probably better this way," I replied. "That scotch was more than I needed."

"You seemed OK with it."

"I was. I think Celia's letter messed me up more than the alcohol."

Devon cocked her head. "What did she say?" She asked. "You don't have to tell me if you don't want to."

I shook my head and smiled. "No, it's OK," I said. "I told Jerry she said more than I could've hoped for and everything I'd wanted to hear."

"That doesn't sound too bad."

"No, but you know how it ends."

"I do. I know. I'm so sorry, Rollie."

"It's not your fault, Dev. It's mine. It's mine for being so stupid."

"Stupid for you know... not being *cautious?*" Devon asked in a whisper.

"No. Stupid for leaving her in the first place," I said. "Going to school and leaving Celia was a huge mistake. I knew it would be. Now I've got nothing but failure to face."

"That's not fair. You didn't know what was going to happen."

"I did. So did Celia. She didn't think I was going to fail, but she knew things would go bad."

"What are you going to do now?"

"Well, tomorrow I'm going to her house. I don't know what's after that."

"I wish you wouldn't go. It's not going to be good."

"Everyone keeps saying that, but they don't say why."

"I guess you have to find out on your own."

"I guess so. Another uncertainty, but it seems to be the only thing I'm sure of."

Devon got up and patted my shoulder. She asked if I needed anything else. I told her no and thanked her for the chat. She smiled and left the room. I remained seated by a cozy, perfect December fire, but all I could feel was cold. Good and bad adrenaline surged through my body as my hormones fought with each other. I couldn't seem to calm down, nor could I shake the fears I had. My insides were in a flux and I began to feel nauseous. The egg nog certainly didn't help. It was delicious, but no longer appealing.

My mom called me into the dining room. I was hesitant to go. However, I felt if I didn't, I'd just cause more problems. I didn't need any more of them today. I got up and joined my family.

"How are you doing?" My mom asked.

"A little better than earlier, but..." I said, trailing off.

"You need to get some sleep. You'll feel better tomorrow."

"I wish that were true, mom. Tomorrow may be even worse."

"You're not really going to the Chandler's house, are you?"

"Yes. I have to."

"It's such a bad idea, Roland."

"I know. You all keep saying that but won't say why. I know it's not going to be pretty, but I have to do it."

"Please reconsider."

"No. Not on this. I can't. I can't rest on my laurels."

"Well, at least think about it, please. I know you're hurting. I don't want to see you hurt anymore. None of us do."

Devon agreed. "Mom's right, Rollie," she said. "You already know what you need to know, why push things?"

"Because of the things Celia said," I responded. "I can't let that go."

My mom sighed. "But Roland, you have to. It's all been done. You can't change the past," she said. "Celia is gone. She's married. Just let her go."

"I already did once mom," I lamented. "And it cost me everything."

"What does that mean?" My mom asked.

"I don't know. I just... Please just let me go, OK? I just have to do this."

"You're going to do what you want, but please, *please just think about it,* OK. Sleep on it. Promise me that, OK?"

"I will. I promise."

My mom asked me to 'think about' going over to the Chandler's. I promised her I would. I kept my promise. I'd thought about it. As I washed out my glass, I thought about how I couldn't wait to go toe-to-toe with that fucking pervert Big Kenny. I thought about how I would let into Tina for slapping Celia and let her know that she was right---*I was* the father of Celia's baby. I thought about how I was going to destroy them, and how much joy I was going to get from hurting them the way they'd hurt us.

See mom, I promised I'd think about it---and I did.

I went to my bedroom and got ready to go to sleep. I took off my clothes and hung them over the desk chair. I put my underwear in the hamper and turned off the light. I curled up naked with Celia's pillow and closed my eyes. Again, I pretended I could smell her in the pillow. I held it tight. I thought about the redemption---no, *the revenge*---I'd get tomorrow. I smiled. I don't remember anything else.

CHAPTER 26

I woke up cold. Celia's pillow was between my legs and that gave me comfort. My feet were hanging out of the bed and the sheets were pulled free from the mattress. Only my hips and Celia's pillow were covered. It was about eight AM.

Like yesterday, everything seemed quiet. I got out of bed, got dressed and went to the den. It was warmer in the den. I sat on the couch. I tucked my feet beneath me and pulled a pillow to my lap. I turned on the TV and watched some cheesy early morning program. It sucked. I'd seen it before when I was younger. I couldn't believe it was still on the air.

I flinched on the couch. I couldn't get comfortable. My mind was racing. I just wanted to rein myself in. I wanted to feel normal. Feeling normal meant feeling nothing.

I got up to take a shower. I didn't shower yesterday at all. I felt filthy. I needed to feel clean. I found towels and a washcloth and soap and shampoo. I went into the bathroom, took my clothes off and got in the shower.

I actually felt like I was being cleansed. The water was the right temperature and it poured over me like a tropical waterfall. I was reminded of the morning I'd showered with Celia at the Sleepy Swan Inn. I could sense her around me. I could feel us making love as the shower rained beads upon us. I got an erection in the shower. I began to masturbate, and I thought about Celia. I tried so hard to come and I couldn't. No matter what I did, I could not ejaculate thinking about her.

I stopped and broke down. I wanted this so bad. I needed it. She told me to do it for her and I couldn't. *I just couldn't.* I don't know why. Was it guilt? Was it anger? Was it a combination of everything bad I was feeling? I tried not to be selfish, but selfishness---vengeful selfishness---was all I felt. I hated my-self right now. Everything I felt was wrong and evil. This was supposed to be a mini-baptism, but instead it had become a hate-filled soaking. The water began to hurt. I tried to fight it. I reached for the valve and turned off the shower.

Everything went white. It was a flash---the kind of flash they say you have during a near-death experience. I looked around and I was in the guest shower at my folks' house. Nothing had changed, I was just wet now.

I toweled off and tried to replay what had just happened. It was to no avail. My focus had not changed. It was not on cleanliness, masturbation or anything purifying---it was still target-sighted on revenge. Unfortunately, it was still too early to act upon anything of the sort.

I got dressed and left the bathroom to go and make myself some breakfast.

My sister came out to the den where I was eating. She bade me 'good morning' and I responded in kind. She went to the kitchen and I heard her pouring a bowl of cereal. When she'd finished, she returned to the den, and we ate together.

"Corn flakes?" I asked.

"Yeah, I'm not feeling the sugar today," Devon replied.

"How are those flakes? Pretty boring?"

"Yeah. Corn flakes are a total drag,"

"You should see the box I designed. It's pretty awesome. It's going to make corn flakes kick ass."

"Anything would help! You have a picture of this revela-tion-creating box?"

"No. I didn't even think about photographing it. My mind was elsewhere. I was just glad to get it done. It's the first assignment I think I've actually finished---and enjoyed doing."

Devon laughed. "Man, I can't believe you're bombing out in school," she said. "Is it really that bad?"

"I hate it. I just can't get into it at all," I said. "I tried to tell mom and dad, but you know... It's just not for me. I don't know what is anymore."

"Mom and dad were so upset when they got the letter saying you were on academic probation," Devon said. "I've never seen dad so torqued off."

"I can imagine. I'm really surprised they haven't brought that up yet."

"Well, something else kind of trumped it. Plus, you've only been here a couple of days. It'll come around."

"Thanks for the warning."

"Any time, big brother!"

We finished eating and took our dishes into the kitchen. We rinsed them and put them in the dishwasher. I looked outside and saw the sky was gray and overcast, but it had not snowed.

"Maybe it won't snow anymore while I'm home," I commented.

"Jerry will be upset," Devon said. "He wants to take Hannah skiing."

"I heard he's a regular *prince of the powder* now."

"Who told you that?"

"He did---well, not in those words. He was bleeding at the airport about the lack of snow."

Devon snorted. She quickly covered her face in embarrassment. "Sorry! I found that hilarious! He sucks!" She said. "He's only been out a couple of times and he spent more time on his bacon than on the skis."

"I kind of figured." I said. "He should take the lack of snow as a sign."

"What kind of sign?"

"One that says: Gerald McCallum---find a new, safer hobby. If he's on his ass that much, perhaps tobogganing may be his gig?"

Devon laughed and tagged my arm. It was that little strike that says: 'you're terrible!' She left the kitchen and went to her room. I stared out the window again.

I looked at the clock and noticed it was approaching

10:30AM. My parents and my brother were still asleep. It seemed odd that they'd sleep so late. I remembered that today was Sunday. Things began to make sense.

I sat and thought about how I was going to handle my 'meeting' with Celia's folks today. I had to figure something out. Yesterday I wanted ultraviolence. I wanted to hurt them so bad and make them suffer for the things they'd done to Celia. I wanted to let them know that I was the father of Celia's baby. Tina claimed she knew, but I wanted her to hear the truth--- straight from my lips and as vindictive as possible. Everything I'd wanted was born of anger, frustration and a newfound disdain for Mr. and Mrs. Chandler.

Now; however, it seemed as if I'd cooled off a little. I was still mad, and still bent on revenge, but not to the degree I had been. Perhaps 'sleeping on it,' did me some good?

I started to wonder if going over to the house was even necessary. It was true what my sister said: I knew what I needed to know. There were still the other issues, though. Those were the things that were gnawing at me and I had to confront them and the people who caused them.

I went to the bathroom and brushed my teeth. When I was finished, I went back to the kitchen to grab my dad's truck keys. He was up and reading the paper.

"Morning Rollie," my dad said. "You sleep OK?"

"Fine. I was pretty tired," I replied.

"You still plan to go into town?"

"Yes. I'd like to go right now if I could."

"Well, your mom and I don't like the idea, but you're bound and determined, so..."

"I just need to clear a few things up, that's all, dad."

"I understand. Your mom does too. We just think you should let it go."

"I know. But I can't. The damage is done, but I just... I just need closure, I guess."

"Interesting way of putting it. Go and do what you have to, son. We'll be here for you when you get home, you know that."

"I do."

I pulled the truck keys off the hook, put on my coat and boots and left the house. It was windy and cold, but not too miserable. I climbed into the truck and cranked it up. The engine sounded good to me. I hadn't driven in such a long time and being in control of a vehicle made me feel alive and free. I drove through the residence and out to the main road.

The radio was on and the song playing was 'All Cried Out' by Lisa Lisa & Cult Jam with Full Force. I turned the song up to torture myself. I love this song, but at this moment, it was plunging daggers into my heart. Celia loved this song, too which made it even harder to bear.

As I drove through town I began to think about Celia's letter. I started to recall a lot of her words and I realized that she mentioned quite a bit about sex, but not anything else regarding intimacy. No 'I miss kissing you,' no 'I miss holding you,' no 'I long to touch you,' it was just 'I miss making love with you,' and 'I think about you when I want to make myself come.'

For as much as I truly missed making love to Celia, I missed everything else even more. I missed kissing her lips and feeling her tongue touching mine. I missed holding her body and trying to get as close and tight to her as possible. I missed caressing her skin; touching her face and looking into her eyes when I did it. I missed holding her hand, feeling her soft palm in mine. I missed the way I could tell how she was feeling by how she held my hand. I missed touching her hair and the way it smelled. I missed the small of her back and the soft, but barely noticeable patch of felt just above her hips that I'd discovered one night while we were making out. She never mentioned any of these things---she just mentioned sex alone. I found I was getting frustrated.

I was getting frustrated because I had turned Celia into something she was not supposed to become. She said I turned her into a 'woman,' but I think it was more than that. I always knew from when we first started dating that beneath that chaste and prudish surface of hers was an animal that yearned to be free. It turns out that *I had* unleashed that animal and now it---*she*---was prowling in someone else's jungle.

She thanked me for doing this for her. I began to hate myself for it. She said I made her stronger. I don't believe I did. I just made her available and accessible.

I made her not afraid to explore her sexuality. I made her confident in her abilities to perform in bed. I did all of these things to her, and now she was performing them with someone else---*someone who wasn't me.* I felt like she was rubbing my face in her marriage and the fact that night after night some other guy was making love to her. She said it was meaningless, but it couldn't be---not unless I'd also turned Celia into a cold-hearted, unfeeling bitch as well as a raging nymphomaniac.

I felt like when she told me about the 'meaningless' sex she was really saying: 'hey, I'm getting fucked every night by 'whatzizname,' and how's by you?' My answer: *I've got nothing. I can't even masturbate and make things happen.*

Celia asked for my forgiveness. I should've asked for hers: *please forgive me for doing this to you. Please forgive me that we ever met. Your life would've been so much better without me.*

I came around the corner and entered the neighborhood where Celia's family lived. I could easily turn back, but no. *I have to do this.* I'm here. I drove the blocks beyond her house. I was so close, but whereas before I was ready to pounce, now I was ready to park the truck and say *I was here* and go home. No. *I've come this far.*

I spent the whole drive rationalizing Celia and what she'd become. I tried to pretend I was over her. She was with another and even my child would be his as well. I didn't exist anymore in her world. However, I still needed to...

I don't even know what I was fighting for anymore. Fuck Big Kenny and his cunt wife Tina. She let him violate her daughters. *She did it.* I can't fix that. He allowed himself to be a despicable, incestuous rapist. *He did it. She allowed him to do it.* I CANNOT FIX ANY OF THIS! I have to go home. My family was absolutely right: *nothing good can come from this.* But I was here. I was a block away. I just needed to...

I pulled into the Chandler's driveway and I felt my blood go cold. This was wrong. I should just leave, but I didn't. I shut the truck off and got out. The house looked different. Maybe it's because it was winter? There were two children playing in the front yard. They were trying to build a snowman from the scant piles of dry snow on the grass.

"That's the wrong kind of snow for that," I told them. "You need the wet stuff. That fat, thick snow works the best."

The kids looked at me like I was nuts. The little girl pulled her scarf from her face and asked who I was and if I was here to see her dad. I didn't know. I didn't recognize these kids and thought I may have pulled up to the wrong house. I looked at the address by the door: *850.* I peered down the street at the sign: *Magnolia Drive North.* This was it---but something was amiss.

A man came out of the house and said 'hello' to me. I responded in kind and apologized to him for parking in his driveway.

"What can I do for you..." he asked, inquiring as to my name.

"Rollie McCallum, sir," I said. "I think I have the wrong house."

"Where are you looking for?"

"850 Magnolia Drive North."

"This is it."

"Um. I'm sorry again, but I have to ask---how long have you lived here?"

"About two months, or so. We bought this place as a foreclosure."

"Oh. Did you know the people who'd lived here before---the Chandlers'?"

"No, not really. We knew they'd lost the house. That's about it."

"Did they leave a forwarding address or anything?"

"No. They just left. Did you know them?"

"Yes sir, I did," I said, as I could feel my eyes well with tears. "They're my child's grandparents. There's an aunt and a couple uncles too."

The man looked at me. He seemed as if he wasn't sure what to say. He invited me in. I declined.

"There were a few things left in the house when we moved in," the man said. "Would you like to see them? Maybe there's something you can use to help find them."

"No, thank you," I said. "I think I just found everything I needed."

"I'm sorry, Rollie."

"No apology necessary. I'm glad to see this house full of love."

The man looked at me again, unsure of what to make of my comment.

I climbed into the truck and started it up. I thanked the man for his time and apologized again for intruding. He smiled and waved goodbye. I sat for a moment as he and his children went into the house. Part of me was hoping he would run outside with something---maybe the cassette I'd made for Celia. *Here, we found this!* That was not to be. The door remained shut, but I still waited. No one came out. I shook my head. It was time to go home.

I drove silent and blank through the neighborhood and out to the main road. I turned and went by the park. I wanted to see the swings. I wanted to feel Celia's presence, even though I knew I would not. I saw the swings. They were knotted together; twisted and gnarled and partially snow-covered. Their rusty chains were crimped, and it looked impossible to free them. What the swings had symbolized had changed. The innocence they'd held and represented was gone. They were now mocking and evil. I could not stand to see them anymore.

When I got to the four way stop, I turned in the opposite direction. I headed to the backway towards town, the way that would take me to the new freeway.

I drove past the neighborhood where Sarah lived. Part of me wanted to stop and see her. The better part of me said 'no' and I continued driving. I argued with myself. I knew that Sarah would know where Celia was. She'd know how to get in contact with her. No. *She doesn't love you anymore. She may say it, but she doesn't mean it. She's married. It's over. Let it go---let* her *go.* I kept driving.

I drove the roads Celia and I took to get to the motel where we'd spent the night together. Everything was different now. There were no changes in road surfaces. There were no landmarks and no signs for U.S 27. There was nothing. I drove fast. Celia wouldn't approve, but I didn't care. The freeway was clear. I sped to a place I thought I knew and pulled off onto the shoulder. A car went by heading the opposite direction.

I parked the truck and got out. I looked around. The trees were felled, and the ground was flat below. The freeway lifted above the land as if it was superior to it---as if it had conquered it. *And it had.* I'd been here. There used to be an exit here. This is where the Sleepy Swan Inn once stood. I looked about and found nothing. There was no trace of the motel at all. This timeless icon---this symbol of *what was* had become another victim of the future, of progress *and what was to be.* It was everything I'd feared. The place where Celia and I had made love for the first time, the place where everything changed for us was gone. I breathed deep and sighed. This was it. That fiber of hope I'd kept was now gone, and with it that happy fragment Celia left for me. I truly had nothing. I got back in the truck and fell to pieces.

I pulled into the driveway at my parents' house and I sat in the truck. I'd cried so much as I sat on the shoulder of the new freeway, but apparently, I wasn't done. No sooner had I shut the engine off did I lose it again. I wept so hard. I'd lost everything. My family told me that nothing good was going to come out of my visiting the Chandler's. They were so right. I just wished they'd been honest as to why. It made no difference. I wouldn't have listened anyway. And now here I am, weeping and ready to feast on a huge helping of crow.

I've never wanted my mommy so much in my life. This was the time when a son fell farther than he'd realized and only the one who could comfort him was the one who'd given birth to him. I felt like a soldier dying in war. I was breaking apart. Only my mother could understand. I needed her now. I just wasn't ready, or strong enough to say the words. My mom opened the door to the house and saw me crying in the truck. I was so afraid to go in. I was so afraid to face everything. My mom knew it. She kept the door open for me. She knew when I was ready to come in. My eyes were red and sore. I fell out of my dad's truck and stumbled to the front door.

I didn't say a word. I ran straight to my room and fell onto my bed.

As I'd done before, I cried into Celia's pillow. This stuffed, slumber-enhancing accouterment was all I had left of her. Even this was of little comfort anymore.

My memories of Celia and our love were tainted and fading. She was no longer mine. She told me she still loved me, but those were just words on paper; words written by a confused girl---a confused girl who was now someone else's wife.

The solace I'd taken in Celia's words was now cold and drifting toward non-existent. She was paying me lip service, while giving her body to another man. It was not even remotely a fair trade.

I wanted to go to sleep. I wanted to fall into a slumber and never wake up. My life was over and there was nothing anyone could say or do to make me think differently. It's one thing to break up. It's another thing entirely to lose the love of your life and the child of yours she's carrying all at once. There's very little in the way of viable cures for that type of heartache.

I pulled my face from the pillow and stared at the bedroom wall. I tried to peer through the paint. Beneath the multiple coats of white were words I'd written on the wall:

affirmations, rhymes and little notes I'd drafted to Celia. Why I was searching for them, I don't know. They were as gone as she was. However, I knew they still remained under that paint. I clutched at any straw I could. I was drowning. It was only a matter of time before the undertow of all this pulled me down completely.

As I searched for remnants of my past, I heard a knock on my door. I didn't respond. The knock got louder. I acknowledged it this time, but with a scowl. Finally, the door opened, and my family invaded my room. Everyone took spots within the space. I felt surrounded. I knew I needed---*I wanted*---this, but I was not going to relent just yet. I had to put up a strong front. I had to show my family I could handle this. They knew I couldn't. They weren't stupid. However, *I was*.

My family didn't say a word. I sat up on my bed with tear-swollen eyes and looked at them like nothing was wrong. They were waiting. I couldn't stay strong any longer. I lost it again. I grabbed Celia's pillow and put my face into it.

"You were right. I shouldn't have gone. How did you know?" I asked, as I wept.

I looked up at everyone and saw the varied emotions on their faces. They ranged from stern to soft, but they were all sympathetic. My mom walked to me and embraced me. She stroked my hair as I cried.

"None of that matters," my mom said. "We told you we'd be here for you."

"They were gone mom," I said, as I cried into the pillow. "They were all gone. The Chandlers'. They were gone."

"We know. They've been gone for a while."

"But why didn't you just tell me that?!"

"Because you wouldn't have listened. No matter what we said, you were determined to go to that house. You had to do this on your own. We knew this whether we liked it or not."

My dad spoke, "Rollie, Celia's dad lost his job shortly after she left home. That family was so troubled."

"It's true," my mom said. "Remember I told you Ricky

Chandler was one of my students?"

"I remember," I said. "What happened? Beyond what I already know---what else was there?"

"I don't know. When the school year started things were fine."

I knew where things went south. "Was it about mid-September when you noticed things changing?" I asked.

My mom nodded. "That's pretty much when it was," she said.

"That's when Celia got thrown out," I said, referring to her letter. "She got married shortly after. That had to have some bearing on all of this."

"Oh, I'm sure it does," my mom said. "However, Celia getting pregnant and all has nothing to do with her father's track record."

"No. It doesn't," I lamented. "But I feel I have to shoulder a lot of the blame."

Devon chimed in, "Rollie, you and Celia---you guys made a mistake. Her dad was so messed up."

"I know, Dev, but still..." I said.

My mom stopped me. "No. Roland Jacob McCallum, you will not bear the brunt of that family's misfortune," she stated sternly. "You and Celia were irresponsible, but you are not to blame for anything else that went on in that house."

"What happened, mom?" I inquired. "Please. I have to know."

"Well, when the school year started, things were OK," my mom said. "Ricky was a good kid, but he had..." she paused.

"Some issues?" I interjected.

"Yes, 'some issues,'" she said. "He was restless a lot, but I figured he was just a hyperactive kid. Things started to slip about the time... well... you know."

"I do," I said.

I closed my eyes. I wasn't sure if I wanted to hear any more, but I had to know. I had to know what my mom had observed with Celia's youngest brother.

My mom continued, "As the days progressed, he got more aloof. When he wasn't drawing inward, he was combative."

"That's why his mother nicknamed him 'Rocky,'" I said. "He was always standoffish."

"Really? I wasn't aware of that," my mom said.

"Yeah. He was a bit of a violent kid. Well, he was *physical.* Let's put it that way."

"Well, I reined him in a bit. Once he'd realized who I was, that made things easier. 'Oh, you're *that* Mrs. McCallum?!' he asked me one day."

"I can imagine. We got on OK, Ricky and I."

"He called you his 'biggest brother' once. That made me smile."

That made me smile too.

"So, everything was fine until things happened with Celia?" she asked. "He must've really looked up to her or something."

I interjected. "No. He didn't. They were always going at one another."

My mom seemed shocked by this. "Really? Why?" she asked.

"She was the first, he was the last. That sort of thing," I said. "I never understood the competition. All of the kids were treated equally: *like absolute shit."*

"I don't know," my mom continued. "But one day Ricky came in disheveled. He was wearing the same clothes he'd had on the day before. This became a regular occurrence."

"Did he say anything?"

"No. He shut down and wouldn't talk to me. After a while, his hygiene became a concern. He smelled bad. He hadn't brushed his teeth. He'd lost weight, too."

"How could you tell? He was a skinny kid."

"Trust me, Roland. Teachers know these things."

"Fair enough."

I could see my mother getting upset. She was devastated that she couldn't help one of her students overcome an obstacle. I knew why she couldn't. What was happening at the Chandler house was beyond repair. Those 'unsettling' things my mom talked about; I knew a lot of them---I'd just found out more.

My mom collected herself and talked again. "One day Ricky came to school with some odd bruises," she said. "They raised red flags with me. I asked him..."

My mother broke down. She could say no more. I started crying again, too. I knew why she was shedding tears. My dad, my brother and my sister had been listening to our conversation but didn't fully understand the entire dynamic of it all.

"Mom, the things Celia said in her letter. They were awful," I explained. "You were seeing a tiny glimpse of what I know."

"Oh my God, Roland. What happened?" My mom asked. "What do you know? What else was going on over there?"

"More than you could imagine and more than you'd ever want to believe," I said. "Celia needed me to be her savior. Her dad bestowed that upon me, too. I didn't... I didn't know..."

I began to cry harder. I felt so weak. I felt like so much had been thrust upon me and I was not able to face the task. *Oh God, I'm so sorry...*

My dad, my brother and my sister converged on my mother and me. They embraced us as we cried. They'd had no idea what was going on before. They had some idea now.

"My God, mom. The things Celia said her dad..." I paused. "...no, that *Big Kenny* did to her and her sister when they were little. They were just little girls..." I said, falling even farther apart.

"THEY WERE JUST LITTLE GIRLS!" I yelled through the tears that cascaded from my eyes. "*THEY WERE JUST LITTLE GIRLS! YOU SICK, TWISTED SON-OF-A-BITCH! HOW COULD YOU DO THIS?!*"

My dad pulled away in shock. He looked at me and grabbed my shoulder. "Rollie, is this why you had to go see the Chandlers'?" He asked.

"Yes, dad. It was. *IT WAS!*" I yelled at him.

"What were you going to do, son?" My dad asked with an eerily, nervous calm.

"I was going to kill Big Kenny," I said, matter-of-factly. "He tried to rape those girls. Dad. He. Oh my God..."

My family was in absolute shock. My mom knew something---but not this much.

I pulled myself together somewhat. "Dad. I wanted to hurt Celia's parents," I said. "I wanted to hurt them like they'd hurt everyone else. I wanted to make her dad pay for what he'd done. Then everything got stacked, piled up... You've got to understand..."

My dad was mortified. I had to believe at this point if he had a couple of firearms, he would've loaded them, gave me one and joined me in my quest to hunt down Big Kenny and Tina and shoot them in cold blood---purely justified cold blood.

My father paced. He didn't cuss. He paced when he was fuming. He was practically stomping. He was mumbling unintelligible things, but I knew they were bad. I knew they were directed at Celia's parents. My sister tried to calm him down. My brother was in such confusion. Jerry had come into my room to show support for his brokenhearted little brother. He had no idea he'd be entering---and getting spun into---a centrifuge of chaos and insanity.

Everyone was a mess. There were no rational thinkers amongst the five of us. It was family crisis as it should be. However, the problems were not really ours. They were residual. If they were anyone's, they were mine---and mine alone. My sister grabbed my hand tight. I acknowledged her with a reciprocating squeeze.

I heard her say through her tears, "Dude, you got this."

"No, I don't, Dev. I never will..." I responded.

I was so broken and devastated. Nothing made sense and at this point---nothing ever would anymore. *Put on a brave face.* That's all I could do.

She... I pretended I barely remembered her name. *She*

never even told me goodbye. *She* never even told me about my baby---what was now *someone else's* baby. *Fuck you.* That's what I say to you, whoever you are, because that's exactly what you said to me. You'll never remember me. You've moved on, but I haven't had the chance yet. It must be nice. I guess I did make you a cold-hearted, unfeeling bitch. *Thank me for that.* I guess that's our legacy. When you take off your clothes and get into bed...

I stopped. I didn't want to think about this or about *her* anymore. I asked my family to give me some time alone. My mom was afraid to leave me by myself. I assured her I was OK, but she was apprehensive. My mom feared I was going to do myself in. The thought *had* crossed my mind, but was it worth it? Kill myself? Over *her?* No way. I wouldn't give *her* the satisfaction. I just needed time. I needed sleep. Tomorrow was not going to be any better, but at least tomorrow, I'd have nothing to deal with. This was the good kind of nothing. It was finally just that---*nothing.*

Everybody left my room and I was alone again, but I didn't *feel* alone. I was just by myself. I took a deep breath. I thought of Samuel Taylor Coleridge's poem *The Rime of the Ancient Mariner.* I thought about how this albatross---*my* albatross named... um... yeah, *whatever*... had dropped from neck.

I was exhausted. I truly needed sleep now. I flipped *her* pillow over and stuffed it beneath mine. I was done. Tomorrow I was going to bleach the pillow and the case. I was going to bleach *her* and *her* lingering stench---perceived as it may be--- right out of it.

There was nothing left of the pillow but a bit of extra support for my neck. *She* was gone. I pushed the pillows together and fell into an erratic sleep. I dreamt a lot. None of it was good. I kept waking up. I just wanted some peace.

CHAPTER 27

I was awoken by the sound of a harsh December wind outside my room. The windows rattled as the gusts stirred and spun and crashed against the glass. The wind howled as if it were in pain and begging to come inside and join me in my sorrow. *Sorry, my friend, I cannot be of any help.* The wind responded in kind and remained in its element, throwing itself against the house and hurting just as I did.

I rolled onto my back and felt a cold ache deep in my bones. My blood was frozen, and I could not move. I did not want to get out of this bed. I knew I needed to leave the confines of my room and walk away from the last shards of memories I'd had of Celia. I'd remembered her name again and it pained me to say it. It pained me to even think it.

The longer I lay in this bed---a bed which Celia had been in---atop a pillow which she had laid her head upon and left her scent, the more I began to think of her again.

I sat up and pulled myself out from beneath the covers. I was dressed in my flannel pajamas. I didn't recall putting them on. Even their warmth was little recourse for the chill I felt within me.

I staggered out to the kitchen. I felt slightly drunk, although I'd had nothing intoxicating to drink. It must've been the residual effects of last night. My brain was still processing everything. My heart was obviously still shattered---that would take a very long time to heal.

My dad was eating a small breakfast. He was alone and reading the paper. I chose not to disturb him and moved toward the den. I needed to talk to my dad. I needed his advice. I would wait. It could wait.

Today was the day I started my life over. What a concept: a re-birth from the worst possible circumstances. When I'd thought about such things in the past, I had always imagined that this re-birth would occur the day I married Celia and we began our new lives as husband and wife. The word *re-birth* sounded sickening to me now. The only re-birth that was occurring was my child being born and handed to another man. That was *his* re-birth, and he knew nothing of it. My new life was beginning with a *de-birth*---a death of sorts.

I couldn't fathom my life without Celia. Now, I had no choice. I saw nothing. It was a blank slate. This should be a good thing, but it was not. Only half the slate was blank, and that was the half which included Celia. The other half was me, as I existed now: severed and searching for this other part of me. I finally went to see my dad.

"Morning, Rollie," he said. "I figured you'd sleep for a while, today."

"No, I couldn't sleep anymore," I said. "The wind woke me up, plus it was time."

"How are you feeling?"

"Better than yesterday, but nowhere near to well."

"That was a lot to take---for all of us. I'm sorry, son. I really am."

"It's OK. I'll survive. What else can I do?"

I poured myself a cup of coffee and offered some to my dad as well. He accepted.

"Remember how I like it, right?" My dad asked.

"A drop of cream and an ice cube?" I wondered aloud.

"That's it."

I served my dad his coffee as requested. I sat down next to him at the table. I sipped my coffee slow. It was too hot. I set it down to let it cool.

"Put an ice cube in that," my dad said.

"I'll wait," I said. "I don't want to water it down."

"It won't be too bad, trust me."

"That's OK, dad. The cube is your thing. I need my own 'coffee trademark.'"

My dad nodded and sipped his coffee. He could tell I wanted to say something. I knew I *had* to say something. I had no idea where to begin. I decided to go with the obvious.

"Dad, I need a new start," I said.

"Well, once you get back to campus, you'll have a jump on that," he replied.

I shook my head. "That's not what I mean," I said.

"What is it then?" He asked.

"I need to start all over. Not here and not at school. I need a truly blank, no---*a clean* slate. I want to drop out of school."

"I don't think that's going to happen," my dad said, matter-of-factly. "It seems too drastic. Too final. There's no way."

"It *is* final," I said. "That's what I want. I want finality."

My dad shook his head. "No, that's not going to work," he stated. "What made you decide this?" He took a long sip of his coffee.

"I'm failing dad. You know this. It's no secret... you've got it in writing," I said. "I'm just going to keep failing when I go back. It'll be even worse."

"How can you fail 'worse'?"

"Send me back to school and you'll see."

Perhaps this conversation would've been better suited for another time. My dad seemed to be having difficulty grasping such a major issue at this early point of the day.

"Dad, I feel like I've been cut in half. I can't get whole like this," I explained. "I need something to take me away from this and start completely anew."

"What do you mean 'cut in half'?" My dad asked.

"OK. I'm here now. This is a *known*. It's one of the few knowns I have," I said. "School is also a known, but it's rife with *unknowns*. It has been from the start. If I go back, it's more of the same. It's worse if I stay here, too."

"That doesn't make sense, Rollie."

"It will, dad, just hear me out, OK?"

My dad sat and listened as I explained the situation. I told him that the only things I was certain of were my family and Celia. School was always a question mark---even before I went. Ironically, Celia was a bit of a driving force behind going to school. I wanted an education so I could get a good job and provide well for her and our family---just as he and mom provided for Jerry, Devon and me. Now Celia was gone. All that she meant to me and all we were destined to have was gone. I had nothing. Before that, school had gone from a question mark to a *nothing* as well. I'd lost my drive and will to perform. I didn't care. Celia's lack of communication and slow---albeit obvious---disconnect made the waning wants I had to excel decrease even more. So, in a sense, school was long gone before Celia. I just needed an excuse to end it.

Now I was trapped in a situation where I'd lost my love, and was being told I needed to return to a place I hated; a place which may be the very thing that killed the flower Celia and I had planted---a place which destroyed us *and* our future. I couldn't go back to that. I'd be essentially returning to the scene of the crime. On the other hand, I am here now---at home, with my family. I feel safe, but I know I cannot stay. To start this new life, I would need a truly fresh start---but not here and certainly *not there*.

"Do you understand why I can't go back, now, dad?" I asked.

My dad looked addled, but I think he was grasping things.

"You might want to think about this a little more," he said. "I hear you and it all makes sense, but it's such a big move."

"I know it is," I said. "But it's what I've got to do."

"I'm not going to say anything right now. We need to sit down with your mom and talk this out, OK? She's not going to be very happy."

"She'll understand when I tell her what I've just told you."

"She's a tough sell, your mom."

"I know, but she also knows how difficult things have been for me. She wanted me to go to school. I tried and I failed.

Additional failure is not a viable option."

"No, it certainly isn't."

"Plus, mom's not gonna' throw her wounded cub into another unknown. The jaws of the wolves await the sickly off-spring; his odor of weakness is their scent of the kill."

My dad shook his head. "Where'd you come up with that?!" He asked.

"I just made it up," I said.

"That's pretty heavy stuff. You might've chosen the wrong art focus."

"I chose the one that seemed the quickest way to a career. See how well that worked."

I poured another cup of coffee for my dad and me. I put a splash of cream and an ice cube in his and added an ice cube to mine as well. He smiled and gave me a 'mug salute.' I sat down and we were quiet for a few minutes.

My dad looked over the paper again and I peered at the pages was well. I missed the paper. I missed writing those tacky high school articles and features.

As I thought about working on the paper, I could smell the faint aroma of shortcakes. I breathed deep to gather more of their scent, but it was not there. It never had been. I felt sad.

My dad looked at me. He asked if I was OK. I told him I was. He went back to reading for a moment.

He spoke again, "Just out of curiosity, what would you do if you left school?"

"I'd join the service," I said. "Without a doubt, I'd enlist."

My dad smiled. It was that 'I knew you'd come around' grin that fathers get when their children realize that dad was right.

"What brought that on?" He asked.

"Well, I figured if I was going to start over, that's the best place. I'll get stripped, shorn and reconfigured," I said. "I'll be a whole, new person. I wouldn't even recognize myself."

"Sounds like that's what you want."

"No, dad. It's what I *need*."

My dad and I talked to my mom. She was not pleased with the decisions I had made, but she knew they were the right ones. My dropping out of school would cost my parents a great deal of money, but no more than my failing already had. We agreed I would return to campus after the holiday break so I could gather my things. I didn't have much. It was symbolic of how I'd felt since the day I started classes---right up to now. Now, I had even less.

I felt good. I felt as if my new choices were the best ones I could make. I wish I'd made them sooner. I was contemplating a new beginning in the one place I swore I'd never go; the one place where had I gone initially, the new life *I thought* I was destined for, would have been easily obtainable.

I thought about Celia. I thought about the book I'd been reading. Talk about life imitating art. I'd identified with the protagonist Jake and Celia had become my Lady Brett Ashley. She'd moved on, and now I was doing the same. She'd found her answer even if it was not the one she'd sought. Again, I was doing the same. She'd found her new freeway and it had taken her elsewhere. It was time for me to drive a new road as well. She'd expressed her troubles to me, but there was nothing I could do to help her. She had someone else to pick her up. I had my own troubles---and I'd have to face them alone. Change and the unfamiliar still scared me, but if Celia could face it like she did, so could I. I'd become weak. I wanted to be strong. *I would be strong again.*

On my way out to see some friends one afternoon before Christmas I spied a bundle of newspapers. My dad had stacked them for additional kindling in the fireplace. I didn't think much of the papers at first. Suddenly, I spotted a headline on one of them that read:

NEW FREEWAY ELIMINATES OLD 27

I closed my eyes for a second. I opened them again, turned and walked away. My new life had indeed begun.

ABOUT THE AUTHOR

Sean Siverly

My writing journey began in high school with mainly short stories, and an attempt at a romance novel.

In 1987, I submitted a short story for a college competition. The story was not selected, but it did give me a fresh perspective on my writing.

While in the Air Force, I took a story from high school and started to re-write it as a novel. Simultaneously, I began working on a horror novel titled 'Overpass.' Both stories remain unfinished.

I pursued my fine arts degree, receiving a BFA in painting in 2002. Even though my primary focus had changed, writing was never far from my mind, as I continued to write short stories and essays.

In 2015, I took up writing as a full-time venture, penning several short stories, novellas and novel-length works based on a variety of subject matter.

BOOKS BY THIS AUTHOR

Excursions With The Chief

Travelogue writer Louis DeCarlo's most recent travels have left him lost and devoid of vision. He needs an adventure.

Enter the Chief: a man who has been there and done that. However, for all he's seen and done, he too has become lost and empty.

Both men are searching for their next great story. They travel from place to place—enjoying life and learning lessons along the way. What ensues is a journey to find not only the key to cracking Louis's dilemma but also the Chief's five elements to happiness.

Printed in Great Britain
by Amazon